Enid Blyton

Three Bold Pixies

...and other stories

Bounty
Books

Published in 2015 by Bounty Books,
a division of Octopus Publishing Group Ltd,
Carmelite House
50 Victoria Embankment,
London EC4Y 0DZ
www.octopusbooks.co.uk

An Hachette UK Company
www.hachette.co.uk
Enid Blyton ® Text copyright © 2011 Chorion Rights Ltd.
Illustrations copyright © 2015 Award Publications Ltd.
Layout copyright © 2015 Octopus Publishing Group Ltd.

Illustrated by Rene Cloke.

ISBN: 978-0-75372-965-6

A CIP catalogue record for this book is available from the
British Library.

Printed and bound by CPI Group (UK) Ltd, Croydon, CR0 4YY

CONTENTS

Three
Bold Pixies

There were once three pixies who were most unhappy in the village where they lived. Everybody was so busy that they had no time to laugh or talk to each other, or have a party. All they thought about was how to make more and more money.

The pixies wanted time to sing and dance and enjoy having friends to visit. So they made up their minds to move away and find a home somewhere else.

"A little red cottage with a white gate and red roses growing round the door would be nice," said the first pixie, who was called Peri.

"No, a little white cottage with a red gate and pink roses," said Patter, the second pixie.

"Oh no, brothers, a pink cottage with a blue gate and white roses," said Pipkin, the third pixie.

So they set off one morning to find

their cottage home. They went down the lane, under the hedge, and across the field. They went through the wood, down the road, and up the hill. And on the other side of the hill they saw a dear little cottage. It had yellow walls, a blue gate, and honeysuckle growing all over it; and although it wasn't exactly like any of the pixies had pictured it, they all thought it would do very nicely.

"But there is smoke coming from the chimney!" said Peri. "Someone lives there. What a nuisance!"

"Well, we'll go and see if they'll let us live there instead," said Patter.

"But suppose they won't let us," said Pipkin. "Suppose there is someone perfectly horrid living there?"

"Dear me, yes," said Peri. "Well, one of us will go first – and if there is someone horrid there, the others can save him if he gets into trouble."

"You go, Pipkin," said Patter. "You are the bravest."

Well, Pipkin went marching up the path to the little front door of the yellow cottage and he banged on the door with

the knocker – *blim-blam, blim-blam!*

"Come in!" said a voice. So Pipkin walked in, and who should he see inside but Clikity-Clok, the bad gnome!

Pipkin didn't like the look of him at all but he was bold and said, "Good-day to you! Can I come and live in this cottage?"

7

"You can!" said Clikity-Clok; and he caught hold of Pipkin and pushed him into a cupboard. He locked the door and laughed. "Aha!" he said. "You won't get out of there, pixie. You can live in this cottage until old wizard Nim-Nam comes and then I'll sell you to him!"

Well, the two pixies who were left outside waited and waited for Pipkin to come back but he didn't. So then Patter

marched boldly up to the front door and banged with the knocker – *blim-blam, blim-blam!*

"Come in!" shouted the gnome – and in went Patter. But when Clikity-Clok saw Patter he looked quite scared. "Stars and moon!" he said. "Didn't I lock you up in the cupboard just now?"

Well, as soon as he heard that, Patter knew what had happened to Pipkin! So he said, as bold as brass, "Yes, you did put me in the cupboard, Clikity-Clok, but I got out as easy as winking!"

"Oh, you did, did you?" said the gnome, and he caught hold of Patter and threw him into a big chest. "Well, you won't get out this time! I'll lock you here safely till the wizard Nim-Nam comes along to buy you!"

Well, Peri was the only one left outside the house now, and he waited and waited for Patter and Pipkin to come back but they didn't. So he too walked up the front path and banged with the knocker – *blim-blam, blim-blam!*

"Come in!" roared the gnome, and in walked Peri. Clikity-Clok leapt to his feet in fright. "Didn't I lock you in the cupboard – and then in the chest – and here you come banging at my front door again!" he squealed.

Then Peri knew what had happened to the others and he grinned at Clikity-Clok and said, "Oh-ho, gnome, you may think you are clever but you can't beat ME!"

The gnome gave a yell and rushed out of the front door to fetch his friend Nim-Nam.

Peri ran quickly to the chest and let out Patter. He opened the cupboard and let out Pipkin. "Stand at the front window, Pipkin," said Peri. "And you, Patter, stand at the back window. I"ll go to the bedroom window. See what Clikity-Clok says when he comes along!"

So each pixie went to a window, and kept behind the curtains to watch for Clikity-Clok. Soon the gnome came along with his friend Nim-Nam. The first thing they saw was Pipkin's cheeky face peeping out of the front window. So they ran round to the back – and, bless us all, there was Patter's cheeky face grinning at them there. And when they climbed up to the bedroom window, there was Peri playing peep-bo with them behind the curtain!

"That pixie is magic!" cried the gnome

in fright. "I locked him up twice, and he came banging at my door a third time – and now he is everywhere at once! I'm going!"

He tore off down the road with Nim-Nam at his heels and he never came back.

As for the three pixies, they settled down in the little yellow cottage very happily. And there they live to this day – Peri, Patter and Pipkin – and you can see them doing their shopping any morning in the village.

But nobody knows which is which for they are as alike as peas!

The Pixies' Handkerchief

The three pixies lived in their pretty little cottage with yellow walls and a blue gate and honeysuckle growing all over it. It was called Pixie Cottage, and whenever anyone went by they were sure to see a pixie face looking out of the window.

But the pixies were all so alike that no one ever knew if it was Peri they were looking at, or Patter or Pipkin!

Now one day Peri got a cold. It was a very bad cold and he wanted a big handkerchief to sneeze into.

"Where is the handkerchief?" asked Peri. You see, at that time the pixies had only one large white handkerchief between them. Nobody knew where the handkerchief was. They looked at one another. They felt in their pockets. They shook their heads.

"I haven't got it," said Patter.

"Nor have I," said Pipkin.

"Well, I keep wanting to sneeze," said Peri, "and it is dreadful not to when I want to so badly. Please do find me the handkerchief."

"We washed it last week," said Patter. "Do you suppose it is still hanging out on the line, Pipkin?"

"I'll go and see," said Pipkin. He ran out to the washing-line. There was a pair of socks there and a table-mat. He stared at them both and then ran indoors again.

"No, it isn't there," he said. "But there is a table-mat there, Patter. Do you think we took down the white handkerchief and used it for a table-mat? We have been using a table-mat but ours is on the line. So we must have been using something else for a table-mat."

"Ooh yes, I remember now," said Patter. "I did use it for a table-mat because the table-mat was dirty. I took it down from the line, ironed it and used it when Mother Hoppit came to tea the other day."

"Then it must be in the drawer with the tablecloth," said Peri, and he went to look. But it wasn't there.

"It isn't there," said Peri. "Whatever did we do with it?"

"Oh, don't you remember?" said Pipkin suddenly. "We couldn't find the duster to dust the mantelpiece one morning. So you got the handkerchief out of the tablecloth drawer and used that."

"Then the handkerchief must be in the duster cupboard," said Patter, and he went to look. But it wasn't there!

"Oh, I know!" said Peri. "I wanted to

shake the kitchen mat and it was so dusty that I tied the handkerchief round my head to keep the dirt out of my hair. Yes – I did. Don't you remember seeing me with it tied round my head? I took it out of the duster cupboard, I remember."

"Dear me, so you did," said Pipkin. "I wonder what you did with it when you took it off your head."

"I hung it up with your hats in the hall, I expect," said Peri.

"That's the sort of silly thing you *would* do," said Pipkin crossly. "I suppose if you ever wore a coal-scuttle on your head, you'd hang it up in the hall afterwards!"

"I'll go and see if it's there," said Patter. So he went to look in the hall.

But the handkerchief wasn't hanging up with the hats.

"It isn't there," he said. "Now who took it out of the hall, and what for?"

"Oooh, I did!" said Pipkin, remembering. "We played blindman's buff yesterday afternoon, didn't we – and I was the blind man first – and I took the handkerchief out of the hall and tied it round my eyes."

"So you did!" said Peri and Patter. "But what became of it afterwards?"

"Patter was the last blind man," said Pipkin. "What did you do with the handkerchief when you took it off, Patter?"

"I gave it to Peri to wave to the bus when it passed by at teatime," said Patter.

"So you did," said Peri. "I remember waving with it, and the bus driver waved back. But it blew out of the window, didn't it?"

"Oh yes!" said Pipkin. "And the dog next door got it and nibbled it. And you ran out, Patter, to get it, and brought it in full of holes – don't you remember?"

"Quite right," said Patter. "The dog almost bit it in half and there were three big holes in it."

"We put it in the laundry basket to be washed," said Peri excitedly. "I remember quite well!"

"It must be there, then," said Pipkin, and he went to look. But it wasn't there.

The three pixies stared at one another.

"I can feel another sneeze coming," said Peri dolefully. "I wish I had a handkerchief to sneeze into."

"Would you like to borrow the tablecloth?" said Patter.

"No," said Peri. "My sneeze would be lost then. A tablecloth is too big for a sneeze."

"Let us try to think what we did with the handkerchief after we put it into the laundry basket," said Patter. "Someone must have taken it out!"

"I did!" said Peri suddenly. "Don't you remember? I ran up the path this morning and tripped on a stone. I fell down –"

"And hurt your knees –"

"And they began to bleed –"

"So I had to get the handkerchief out of the basket!"

"And we tore it in half –"

"And Patter bound up your left knee –"

"And Pipkin bound up your right knee –"

"And as my knees are not yet better, the handkerchief ought to be tied round them this very minute," said Peri.

"Turn up your blue trousers and we

will see," said Patter. So Peri turned up his blue trousers – and there, binding up his hurt knees, was the handkerchief, in two pieces!

"We've found it!" said Patter.

"Hurrah!" said Pipkin.

But Peri looked gloomy.

"What's the matter?" said Pipkin. "Aren't you pleased that we've found the handkerchief?"

"Not very," said Peri. "How can I sneeze into a handkerchief that is tied round my knees?"

"You can bend over," said Patter.

"When I bend over, my sneeze goes," said Peri, with a long face. "I do want to sneeze. It is simply dreadful to have to keep on not sneezing."

They all started at one another. And then Pipkin had a marvellous idea.

"Let's buy another handkerchief!" he cried. "Why didn't we think of it before?"

"Of course!" said Patter and Peri, cheering up. So off they went to the shop and bought a beautiful white handkerchief for Peri.

So now he is happy. You can hear him sneezing all day long – "A-tish-oo, tish-oo, tish-oo!" But I expect the handkerchief will be lost soon and what a fuss there will be again!

The Squabblers

Did you ever hear the tale of Snap, Snarl and Sneery? It's really rather funny.

As you can tell by their names, they were not very good-tempered goblins. They lived together in a little cottage, and all day long they snapped and snarled and sneered. It was really dreadful to hear them.

Old Mr Kindly lived next door to them and it was very lucky for him that he was deaf, or he would have been most upset to hear them squabbling all day through. But when he left his cottage and went to live with his sister somebody else came to live there – and she wasn't deaf at all!

She was Dame Sensible, a good-hearted, bustling old woman, always ready to help anyone. She was just as good-tempered as the goblins were bad-tempered.

She couldn't believe her ears when she heard the squabblers next door!

"I tell you I didn't!"

"You did. You're a storyteller!"

"Who's a storyteller? I've never told a story in my life."

"Oooooooooh! What a fib!"

"Well, what about you? Who took my sweets when I left them on the mantelpiece?"

"I didn't!"

"You did. You're a storyteller."

Dear, dear – it went on like that all the time and as the goblins had very loud voices Dame Sensible simply *couldn't* help hearing every word. The goblins even woke up in the middle of the night and squabbled about who had the most bedclothes!

"You've pulled all the clothes off me!"

"I didn't. That was Snap. He turned over and dragged them off. Anyway, it's a warm night."

"It isn't. It's bitterly cold."

"Ooooh, fibber!"

"All right. If you think it's so warm, you can give me your share of

the blankets then."

"Oh, you horrid thing! I haven't got a single cover over me at all. Give them back."

Then there would come the sound of a tremendous fight, and Dame Sensible would stuff her fingers in her ears and wish and wish that her neighbours would stop quarrelling and let her go to sleep.

She complained about the quarrelling to people in the village.

"Oh, those three squabblers!" she said. "I wish I could stop them. Has anyone ever tried?"

"Oh, there's only one thing to bring them to their senses," said Mr Gomp, "and that's a good slap."

Dame Sensible was rather shocked. She didn't believe in slapping people. "But surely there is a kinder way of curing them?" she said.

"Well, you find it, then," said Mr Gomp.

Next door the goblins were squabbling again, and she could hear them shouting in their usual tiresome way.

"I didn't!"

"You did!"

"I tell you I didn't!"

She went to see them.

Snap opened the door. "Good afternoon," he said, quite politely.

"Good afternoon," said Dame Sensible.

"I've come to say that I can't bear to hear you squabbling all the time like this. I'm sure that if you know it makes me unhappy you will stop."

"Of course!" said Snap at once. "I'm quite willing, Dame Sensible."

"So am I," said Snarl.

"Me too," said Sneery.

Dame Sensible felt very pleased indeed. "There now! I *thought* you'd all stop that dreadful quarrelling if I asked you," she said.

"I *never* quarrel," said Snap. "It's these other two. You wouldn't *believe* how annoying they are, Dame Sensible."

"*Oh!* How dare you say that!" cried Snarl.

"You dreadful fibber!" cried Sneery "Who began the quarrel this morning – the one about the milk? And who ..."

"Hold your tongue," said Snap, at once.

"What do you mean, hold my tongue?" shouted Sneery. "I shan't."

"Oh, do hush," said poor Dame Sensible, putting her hands up to her ears. "Now listen to me. If you could just *once* go for a whole day without squabbling you would find out how pleasant and peaceful it is – and you would never quarrel again!

Wouldn't that be nice?"

There was a silence. The goblins looked at Dame Sensible. "What will you give us if we do manage to go for a whole day without squabbling?" asked Snap, artfully. He could see a way of getting something for nothing. This kind old lady looked as if she would be ready to give them a nice present!

"Well, listen," said Dame Sensible, taking out her purse. "I want a quiet day tomorrow because I'm making a special spell. It would be worth three whole pounds if you can manage not to squabble. So look – there's one up on the shelf for Snap if he doesn't quarrel. And one for Snarl if he manages not to squabble too. And one for Sneery. I'll come in tomorrow evening and see if you've earned them."

She went out smiling. She was sure that would do the trick. The goblins would certainly keep their tempers for the sake of spending a whole pound each. It was a lot of money to them.

Now, the goblins meant to earn those pounds. What an easy way of earning money – just to stop squabbling for one day. Ha – they could all do that! The next morning they all sat down to breakfast and gave each other little smiles. Then they looked at the shelf where the pounds were, and they winked at one another.

"Easy money!" said Snap.

"Rather!" said Snarl. "I know what I'm going to spend *my* pound on. A bag of toffees! Oooh!"

"Just like you!" said Sneery, in a sneering voice. "Bang goes your pound on something to eat – and that's the end of it. I shall buy some eggs and put them under the hen – then later on I shall get chicks from the eggs and make a lot of money."

"You always did think too much of making money," said Snap. "I shall spend my pound on a new red cap."

"Red! How horrible! It won't suit you a bit!" said Snarl at once.

"Yes, it will. And let me tell you this – I'm spending my pound how I l ike without any advice from *you*," said Snap angrily.

"You're squabbling!" said Snarl at once.

"I am *not*," said Snap. "Anyway, it takes two at least to make a quarrel – so if I'm squabbling, you must be squabbling too. Ha-ha!"

"Ha-ha back!" said Snarl, rudely. "What with you buying a red hat and Sneery buying eggs, I feel I'm living with two big sillies. And I shan't offer you any of my toffees either. Not even a teeny-weeny little one!"

"You're mean and you're greedy and always were," said Sneery.

"I'm not," cried Snarl, indignantly. "You are, I tell you, and don't shout at *me*!" cried Sneery. "Do you know what you're doing – you're quarrelling, see? You won't get your pound."

"I shall," said Snarl. "I shall take it now and put it into my pocket."

"I shall tell Dame Sensible you've quarrelled and quarrelled and quarrelled!" said Snap, joining in.

"And she will give Sneery and me your pound between us."

"She won't. It's in my pocket," said Snarl, with a grin.

Sneery and Snap flung themselves on him and threw him on the floor. In a second they had his pound. He hit out at them and howled.

"You're a naughty, quarrelsome goblin!" said Snap, severely. "And you *shan't* have your pound. So there!"

And do you know, he went to the window, opened it and threw the pound away as far as ever he could!

That was too much for Snarl! He rushed to the shelf, got hold of the other two pounds there and threw *those* out of the window, too!

"There go yours as well!" he squealed.

All three glared at one another and then there was the sound of slaps and thuds and biffs as they all fought together, calling one another names.

They got tired at last and went out into the garden to look for the pounds. But they couldn't find them, which wasn't a bit surprising, because they had all gone over the wall into Dame Sensible's garden!

They felt rather uncomfortable when they couldn't find the pounds. What would Dame Sensible say? What should they tell her?

Dame Sensible happened to be out in the garden when the three pounds came over the wall, and one of them hit her on the cheek. She was most surprised and very much annoyed. She had heard the quarrelling, of course, and had quite made up her mind that the three squabblers were not going to have

those pounds – and dear me, there were the coins flying over the fence, one after the other.

She marched straight into the goblins' cottage. Snap, Snarl and Sneery smiled at her nervously.

"We haven't squabbled yet," said Snap, untruthfully.

"Not once," said Snarl.

"Aren't we good?" said Sneery.

31

"Where are the pounds then?" said Dame Sensible, looking at the shelf.

"Dear me – are they gone?" said Snap, pretending to be surprised. "I can't *imagine* where they are."

"Well, I can tell you," said Dame Sensible, opening her purse. "They're in here. Three shouting, quarrelsome goblins called Snap, Snarl and Sneery lost their tempers and flung them out of the window – and they fell in my garden and I picked them up. I shall not give them to you, of course."

"Oh, you *are* mean!" said Snap. "You promised us a reward."

"You shall have a reward all right," said Dame Sensible, grimly. "A reward for quarrelling, not for being good-tempered. Kindness isn't any good for people like you. Come here, Snap." And she gave him a sharp tap on the hand.

And goodness me, you should have heard the howls that went up from Snap, Snarl and Sneery when they felt the hard, horny hand of old Dame Sensible. They really did feel sorry for themselves.

"Now you listen to me," said Dame Sensible. "I live next door to you and I like peace and quiet. I shall come in and slap you every time you disturb me! If you want to squabble, you can squabble in whispers. Is that quite clear?"

It was. Snap, Snarl and Sneery nodded mournfully. Oh dear – to think they'd lost those pounds and earned a slap instead – how very, very foolish they had been.

Dame Sensible went to the door. "Now remember," she said, "squabble all you like, I shan't try to stop you – but if I HEAR you I'll come marching in!"

The three goblins were upset and scared. To think that Dame Sensible could be so fierce! And yet she had tried to be kind to them and offered them those pounds. It was all their own fault.

"Perhaps we'd better not quarrel any more," said Snap, at last.

But it isn't so easy to stop once you have got into the habit of squabbling. And now, if they want to lose their tempers and say horrid things, they

have to say them in a whisper, in case
Dame Sensible hears – and you know,
it's very, very difficult to be terribly
angry in whispers.

And so I rather think Snap, Snarl and
Sneery will have to give up quarrelling
soon, because really it's impossible to
quarrel in a whisper – and one of these
days I expect Dame Sensible will come
in and give them those three pounds.

I think her name suits her, don't you?
She really is very, very sensible.

The Three Pixies' Birthday

Peri, Patter and Pipkin, the three pixies, were getting excited. Soon it would be their birthday! How exciting!

"It's on Saturday!" said Peri.

"This week!" said Patter.

"Presents for each of us!" said Pipkin, rubbing his hands in glee.

"Have we sent out all the invitations to the party?" said Peri.

"Every one," said Patter.

"And ordered the cakes too," said Pipkin. "What fun we shall have in our little cottage on Saturday!"

"I shall watch for the postman," said Peri.

"I shall find the scissors ready to open the parcels he brings!" said Patter.

"I shall buy some notepaper to write our thank-yous on," said Pipkin.

Peri went to the calendar and tore off a day. "Tuesday today!" he said, reading what the next bit of calendar said. It was a tear-off one – you tore off a sheet each day, and underneath was the next day, waiting. It was Peri's job to do the tearing-off and he never forgot.

The next day he tore off another bit. The birthday was coming nearer! They began to feel excited. Peri always tore off the bit of calendar in the evening before they went to bed, so that they might see what the next day was. And then, one night when he tore the day off, he gave a shout. "Saturday! Tomorrow will be Saturday! The calendar says so. It will be our birthday tomorrow! Hip, hip, hurrah!"

"How happy we shall be!" said Patter.

"I shall wake up early!" said Pipkin.

They went to bed happily. They each did up a parcel for the others. Peri had a red scarf for Patter and Pipkin. Patter had a yellow handkerchief for Peri and Pipkin. Pipkin had a box of peppermints for Peri and Patter. What fun!

They woke up early. "Many happy returns of the day!" they shouted to one

another. "Here's a present for you!"

They each opened their presents and soon Peri and Pipkin were shaking out their beautiful yellow handkerchiefs, and Patter and Pipkin were tying red scarfs round their necks, and Peri and Patter were handing round peppermints.

"It's pouring with rain," said Peri suddenly, looking out of the window. "It's not at all birthday weather."

"Never mind," said Patter. "It may clear up by the time the party comes along. It isn't till this afternoon."

"I can see the postman, I can see the postman!" shouted Pipkin. "I wonder how many cards he has for us!"

"Has he got a lot of parcels?" yelled Peri, nearly falling out of the window as he tried his hardest to see. But the postman had gone into someone's house. Patter pulled Peri back.

"Don't lean out so far," he said. "Do you want to fall out and stand on your head in the middle of the wallflowers?"

"Hurry up and get dressed before the postman comes!" shouted Pipkin, galloping round the bedroom and trying to find his trousers.

They were all so excited that they found it very difficult to dress properly.

"You've got my shoes on," said Peri to Patter.

"Oh, oh, where are my trousers?" wailed Pipkin, and everyone began to look for them, but they were nowhere to be found.

"Patter, you've got two pairs on!"

Peri said suddenly. "You've put Pipkin's trousers on as well as your own. Whatever are you thinking of?"

Well, at last they were dressed, and they ran downstairs just as the postman walked up the path! They opened the door and crowded out. The postman looked surprised to see them.

"What's the excitement?" he said.

"We want to know how many cards and parcels you've got for us!" said Peri.

The postman felt in his bag. "I've got one letter," he said. "It looks like a bill. There are no parcels."

The three pixies stared at one another in the greatest dismay No birthday cards! No birthday parcels! There must be some mistake.

"Look in your bag again, please, postman," begged Patter, nearly in tears.

The postman looked hard. "No," he said, "I haven't anything for you at all except this letter."

Patter opened it. "It's the bill for my new hat," he said. The postman went down the path. The three pixies went inside and shut the door. They looked at

one another sadly.

"Not a single card!" said Pipkin, and he burst into tears. It was a good thing he had a new yellow handkerchief to dry his eyes

"Nobody likes us," said Patter in a trembly sort of voice.

"Nobody has thought of us," said Pipkin, and he sniffed a big sniff. It was all very upsetting and disappointing.

"Never mind," said Patter at last. "Perhaps when our friends come to our party this afternoon they may bring us a card or two, and maybe even a little present. You never know."

"It isn't that we want the presents themselves so badly," said Peri, with another enormous sniff, "it's only that it's so nice to be remembered and loved. It's horrid to think that no one likes us enough to send us even a birthday card."

"If people are not nice enough to do that I don't want them at my party," said Pipkin, suddenly looking very cross.

"That's silly," said Patter at once. "If people are not nice to us that's no reason why we should be horrid to them! We should be as bad as they are then. No, no, Pipkin, we'll welcome them all to our party this afternoon, and not say a word about our disappointment. We think we are very nice, but maybe other people don't. We must just try to be a bit nicer, that's all!"

So that afternoon the three pixies dressed up in their best clothes and set the table for tea. It was still pouring with rain, and at the very last minute Patter came rushing in from the kitchen, very upset.

"I say, I say!" he cried, "what about the cakes? I can't find them!"

"They haven't come!" said Peri and Pipkin. "Oh dear, oh dear, they haven't come! And there's no time to go and get them, and it's pouring with rain; whatever shall we do?"

"We'll wait till all our guests are here and we've said good afternoon," said Patter, "and then you, Peri, must slip off to the baker's with our big umbrella and collect the cakes. We can play games till you come back. Don't drop the big birthday cake now, will you? You'd find it very difficult to pick it up if you did!"

"It's four o'clock," said Peri. "I wonder if anyone is coming. I'll look out of the window."

He pressed his nose against the glass. Nobody was to be seen at all. The time went on, and still no one came down the street. The three pixies began to feel very miserable. What a dreadful birthday!

"Here's someone!" yelled Patter suddenly. So it was – it was old Mr Come-Along, carrying a huge yellow umbrella.

But he didn't come in at their gate – no, he passed right by. He was going to post a letter. The pixies watched him slip it into the pillar box over the way.

"Oh, I do think people are horrid!" said Patter at last, when the clock struck five. "Not a single card, not a single present, and not even a single person to the party, even though everyone accepted. I suppose they don't like us enough to come out in this dreadful rain."

The three pixies had a sad tea all by themselves. Pipkin was very angry about it all, but Peri shook his head.

"Listen," he said, "if people treat us like this there must be something wrong with us. Perhaps we are not kind enough or generous enough. Don't let us feel angry, because that will make us worse. Let's forget about it all and try to be even nicer to everyone, so that perhaps next year they will send us a birthday card each and come to our party."

"Anyway, it's a good thing the cakes didn't come," said Patter gloomily. "That's the only bright spot about today."

"I'm going to bed," said Pipkin. "I'm

tired of this birthday."

"Have one of my peppermints, Pipkin?" said Peri. They all went upstairs sucking peppermints. Before they went, Peri tore off another sheet of the calendar. Saturday went into the wastepaper basket and Sunday came on the calendar.

"Sunday!" said Peri. "Best clothes tomorrow, everybody!"

They took off their clothes in silence, said goodnight, and got into their beds. All three were thinking the same thing: I will be as nice as possible in the future, then perhaps people will like me better. Poor little pixies.

They woke up early next day. The sun shone brightly into their bedroom. They jumped up and dressed and didn't say a single word about the day before. And, to their very great surprise, just as they went downstairs, there came a thundering knock at the front door – *rat-a-tat-a-tat-tat!*

"It can't be the postman!" said Patter in surprise. "He doesn't come on Sundays." They opened the door, and it *was* the postman, grinning all over his red face, too! In his hands he held a bundle of cards and letters.

"Plenty of post today for you!" he said. "Wait a minute. I've got some parcels, too – Mr Peri Pixie, Mr Patter Pixie and Mr Pipkin Pixie. And here are a few more – The Three Pixies, The Pixie Family, and a whole heap more. My, it must be your birthday! Many happy returns of the day!"

"But our birthday was yesterday," said Patter, puzzled. "And why are you here on Sunday, postman? You never come on Sundays!"

"Whatever are you talking about?" said the postman, staring at Patter in astonishment. "Today is Saturday, not Sunday. Ho, ho, ho! So that's why you've got your best clothes on! You thought it was Sunday but it isn't!"

The pixies stared at each other in amazement. Was the calendar wrong then? It couldn't be that, for calendars are always right! Pipkin suddenly gave a squeal and ran to the wastepaper basket. He picked up the sheet that Peri had torn off two days before, but it wasn't one sheet, it was two!

"Peri, you silly-billy-pixie, you tore off two days instead of one on Thursday!" shouted Pipkin, dancing round and round. "You made yesterday Saturday instead of Friday, but it was really only Friday! You tore off two days instead of one! Hurrah, hurrah, hurrah, our birthday is today!"

So it was; oh dear, how happy they were! They looked at their beautiftil cards – twenty-one of them; they opened their birthday letters – fifteen of them; and then they opened their parcels – twelve of them!

"A tin of toffee!" squealed Peri. "And a book about aeroplanes!"

"A pair of blue socks and a new watch!" shouted Patter.

"A tin of biscuits and a red torch!" yelled Pipkin, offering everyone a biscuit. Oh dear, the excitement of it all, especially as they had thought their birthday had been quite missed out by everyone!

"Here are the cakes coming!" shouted Peri, as he saw the baker's van at the door. They fetched them in and oh, the birthday cake was wonderful! It had candles all round and little pixies, made of sweets, round the sides. There were chocolate buns, too, and ginger biscuits and iced cakes. What a lovely party they were going to have!

And they did, too, for everybody turned up, of course, and you should have heard the shrieks and giggles and

shouts! The sun shone brilliantly and everything was perfect.

"It's been a lovely birthday," said Peri, as he cleared away after the party.

"The loveliest one we've ever had," said Patter, sucking a toffee.

"And people do like us after all!" said Pipkin happily. "I'm glad we didn't say horrid things last night when we were so disappointed. We should have been ashamed of ourselves today when everyone was so kind!"

I *am* glad they had a good time after all, aren't you?

Wisky, Wasky
and Weedle

Once upon a time there were three gnomes called Wisky, Wasky and Weedle. Wisky was small, Wasky was tall, and Weedle was fat. They were lazy, mischievous rascals, and they lived in a tiny cottage called Chimneys.

Now one day when Wisky wanted to go out to buy sausages for dinner, he found there was no money at all in the purse they kept on the mantelpiece. He turned it inside out and showed it to the others. "We've got to do some work," he said. "No money, no sausages!"

They sat down on their stools to think hard. Presently Wisky grinned and slapped his knee. "I've got a good idea!" he said.

"What?" asked the others.

"We'll borrow Mr Sooty's chimney-brushes," said Wisky, "And we'll go to the next town where nobody knows

us. I will be the sweep and sweep the
chimney; but I'll be sure to make
a dreadful mess of the carpets and
everything before I go – and that's
where *you* come in, Wasky!"

"Go on," said Wasky.

"You see, as soon as I have left, and
the lady is grumbling about the soot
all over the place, *you* come up, Wasky,
with brooms and dusters and cloths, and
say you are a cleaner. So you get the job
of going in and cleaning the house."

"And where do I come in?"
asked Weedle.

"Well, before Wasky goes, he leaves
the taps running," said naughty Wisky,

with a giggle. "Then, just as the water is running over everywhere and the lady is trying to get a plumber to come in and put things right, *you* come along, Weedle, and say you are a handyman and can do any job like that. You turn off the taps, clear up the mess, take your pay and join us! Now isn't that a good idea? We each make a job for the other, you see."

"Come on, then," said Wasky, getting up. "You go and borrow Mr Sooty's brushes, Wisky."

Very soon, with chimney-brushes, ordinary brushes, and dusters and cloths and a bag of tools, the three gnomes went over the hill to Fiddle-dee-dee, the next town. They looked about for a house where the smoke from a chimney was very black, for they knew that perhaps that would want sweeping – and very soon they saw one.

"Look, there's a chimney that wants sweeping!" said Wisky, pointing to it. "Now, I go first."

Off he went to the back door, carrying his sweep's brushes over his shoulder.

He rang the bell. A sharp-faced little brownie-woman came to the door.

"Good morning, madam; your chimney wants sweeping and I'm the man to do it for you," said Wisky, taking off his cap.

"Are you clean in your work, and quick?" asked the brownie-woman. Wisky said he was – and she led the way indoors to the sitting-room where a fire was burning. She put it out and told Wisky to sweep the chimney and not make a mess.

Wisky fitted together his chimney-brushes and pushed them up the chimney. He meant to make a fine old mess, of course – but, dear me, he didn't need to try and make one! That chimney was almost choked up with soot and, as soon as Wisky's brush moved it, a great pile of fine black soot fell down the chimney, bounced on the hearth and covered Wisky from top to toe! He began to cough and splutter. The soot flew out into the room and settled everywhere – my, what a mess there was!

Wisky took a look at it. He felt

frightened. He hadn't meant to make quite such a mess as that! He stuck his head up the chimney to see if there was any more soot there – and another lot fell all over him! Well, he really did look a sight.

"I'd better stop this," thought Wisky. I'll put my brushes together and go and ask for my money. I'm really sorry for Wasky! He *will* have a mess to clear up!"

He went into the kitchen. When the brownie-woman saw him she gave a scream.

"Oooooooh! What are you?"

"I'm the chimney-sweep, madam," said poor Wisky.

"Well, you want a wash," said the brownie-woman, and she took hold of Wisky by his hair and popped him just as he was into a tub of hot soapy water she had nearby, ready for her washing. My goodness me! What a shock for Wisky! But that wasn't all. When she had finished washing him she took him out into the garden and pegged him up on the line by his coat-collar to

dry. Poor Wisky!

Now Wasky and Weedle were waiting outside, and when Wisky didn't come out, Wasky was cross.

"He's slipped out the back door with his money and gone home," said Wasky. "It's too bad. Well, I'm going in to do my share, Weedle. You'll be next."

He went and knocked at the door. The brownie-woman opened it, looking worried and upset, for she had just seen the terrible mess in her sitting-room.

"Any cleaning you want done, madam?" asked Wasky, showing his brooms and dusters. "I'm the man for

you, if you've got a dirty room you want turned out!"

"Well, it just happens I *do* want someone," said the brownie-woman. "I've had a sweep here and he has left the sitting-room in such a mess that I really don't know what to do about it. Come in."

In stepped Wasky and went to the sitting-room, grinning, but when he saw the truly dreadful black mess that Wisky had left, he turned quite pale. What, clean up all that? Good gracious, it would take him hours and be too much like real hard work! But he had to set to work.

Now Wasky had no real idea how to clean a dirty, sooty room, and he set to work to sweep up the soot with his biggest brush – and, of course, the soot flew up into the air and made more mess than ever! Wasky got desperate – he swept and he swept – and the soot flew and flew. It got into his eyes – and his nose – and his mouth – it flew from the sitting-room into the hall and up the stairs. Wasky made the mess twice as bad, and was quite frightened when he suddenly caught sight of himself in the glass.

"Gracious me!" he said. "How dreadful I look! I think I'll just turn on a few taps so that there is a nice watery mess for Weedle to clear up – and then I'll ask for my money and go."

He went up to the bathroom and turned on all the taps he could see. Then he shut the bathroom door and went downstairs. But before he could even open his mouth to ask for his money, the brownie-woman gave a shriek!

"What! Another dirty gnome to wash!" she cried. "What a dreadful mess you are in!"

She popped Wasky into the tub of soapy water and soon he too was out on the line, hanging there in the wind beside Wisky!

Weedle was waiting outside the house, wondering why Wasky didn't come out. At last he went to the door and rang the bell, just in time to hear the brownie-woman shouting for help.

"Something's gone wrong with the water! The water is pouring down the stairs! Help! Help!"

Weedle went in with his bag of tools. "Madam, I am a plumber," he said. "I will soon put things right for you."

He rushed upstairs and turned off the taps. My goodness, you should have seen the bathroom! The bath was full and overflowing and so was the basin. There was water swirling about the floor, running out on to the landing, into the bedroom and down the stairs! What with the black soot everywhere, and the water, there was a fine old muddle!

Suddenly, Weedle slipped and fell – *splash!* into the water. "Oooooooomph!"

he said, as he swallowed the sooty water.

"Oooooooomph! It's down my neck! It's in my boots! It's all over me! Help! Help! I'm drowning! I can't swim!"

He tried to get up but fell over again – and suddenly slid down the stairs with the pouring water and landed – *ker-plunkity-plunk!* – at the bottom. There the brownie-woman stood, with rubber boots on, trying to sweep the water out of the back door.

"Bless us all!" she said, as she caught hold of Weedle by the hair and shook him well. "Here's another to go on the line."

And would you believe it, she took Weedle and pegged him up on the line to dry too! There the three gnomes hung in the wind, swinging to and fro, wishing and wishing they had never thought of playing such tricks on anyone!

The brownie-woman swept her house out and dried it. She cleaned away the soot and opened the windows to let the air in. And then she took a carpet-beater and she went to the line where Wisky, Wasky and Weedle hung, and gave them

all the hardest thrashing they had had in their lives.

"You are three rogues!" she said, as she unpegged them. "I can see through your tricks. Now go home and make up your minds to do better – or I'll come and peg you up on my line again, as sure as my name is Dame Slip-Slap."

Poor Wisky, Wasky and Weedle! I feel sorry for them – but it served them right all the same, didn't it?

A Muddle
of Pixies

Once the three pixies, Peri, Patter and Pipkin, decided to go for a walk to Bumble-Bee Common. Peri wasn't quite ready so Patter and Pipkin said they would start off without him, and Peri would catch them up as soon as he could.

So off went Patter and Pipkin, arm-in-arm, merrily singing their favourite song. The sun was shining brightly and they were *so* happy.

Now, as they went through the village, little Edward, the fat teddy bear who lived in Bruin Cottage with his father and mother, came tearing down the street on his new scooter. When he saw the two pixies taking up nearly all the pavement he tried to stop – and he couldn't. He wobbled dreadfully, trying to stop himself from going into a pixie – but it was no use.

Thud – bang – kerplonk! The scooter ran into Pipkin and knocked him flat

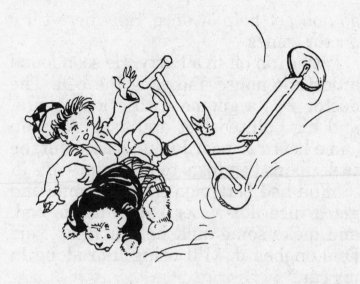

on his back. Patter was all right, though he got a shock. Edward the bear rolled into the gutter, but he was so fat that he wasn't hurt at all. The scooter ran on down the hill and went straight into Goody Two-Shoes' shoe shop, which gave her a dreadful fright.

Pipkin didn't get up. He just lay there, making queer sorts of grunts and groans, and Patter was quite frightened. "You've hurt your knee," he said to Pipkin. "And you've bumped your head! And you've hurt your shoulder too, I think! Oh, poor Pipkin! No, don't try and get up! I'll go and get help at once. Stay here till a doctor comes."

Patter ran off in a hurry. He soon found a doctor's house and rang the bell. The doctor was a gnome with a long beard, and big pointed feet and ears. As soon as he heard of poor Pipkin's accident, he took up his bag to go to help him.

"You had better go straight home and get a nice hot-water bottle in his bed, and make some milk hot for him," said Dr Longbeard. "I'll bring him along in my car."

Patter was very grateful. He ran home at once, taking a short cut, so he didn't see Pipkin again. He knew the doctor would be where Pipkin was in a few moments.

Now Pipkin did not like lying flat in the road. It was very hard. So he sat up. He found that he wasn't so badly hurt after all! His shoulder was still sore, his head had a bump, and his knee was grazed – but really, he wasn't very bad!

"I shall get up and go home," he said. "I can walk, if I limp a bit. Patter was silly to go rushing off to a doctor like that."

So off went Pipkin, limping home.

Now Peri, who had been left at home clearing up, had soon finished his bit of work and set off after the others. He had with him his collection of postcards and he was looking at them as he went. Suddenly they slipped out of his hand and down they went into the road! Peri knelt down to pick them up.

And at the very same moment Dr Longbeard, who was driving along in his car, looking out for a pixie somewhere in the street, saw Peri on his knees in the road.

"There's the poor old hurt pixie!" he said to himself. "Hasn't even been able to stand up yet! Well, I'll soon put him right!"

He stopped the car and jumped out. He hurried to Peri, who looked up in surprise.

"Just let me bandage your head up first," said Dr Longbeard, and he took out a big white bandage. "Where's the bump? Dear, dear, you've such a lot of hair that I can hardly feel your head through it! Never mind – if I bandage

the whole of your head that's sure to include the bump!"

"I don't want my head bandaged," said Peri in alarm, wondering whatever the doctor was doing.

"No, no, I'm sure you don't," said the doctor. "Now, now, be brave, be brave! I'll rub your shoulder next. You may have sprained it."

"I don't want my shoulder rubbed," said Peri, getting cross. "Oooh! You hurt! Don't rub so hard!"

"Dear, dear, does it hurt very much?" said Dr Longbeard. "Well, you must have had a very hard fall, yes, you must.

Now for the knee."

"I don't know what you're talking about," said Peri angrily, and he tried to jerk his leg away from Dr Longbeard. "Don't do it – what are you tying my leg up for? Oh, you've done it so tightly that I can't walk!"

"Poor fellow, poor fellow," said the gnome. "Here is a crutch to lean on. You'll soon be all right now!"

Very angry indeed, poor Peri was bundled into the doctor's car and driven home. When he got there the doctor bustled out and went to the door. "Have you got the bed ready, and the hot milk?" he called to Patter.

"Yes, bring him in!" shouted Patter. Then up the path, hopping along with his crutch, came poor puzzled Peri, wondering if everyone was quite, quite mad.

Patter met him at the door – and he stared and he stared.

"But Peri," said Patter, "I thought it was Pipkin that had had the accident, not you! Am I mad? Surely it was Pipkin!"

"Everybody's mad," said Peri. "I was just picking up some postcards I'd dropped when along came this doctor fellow and bandaged my head and pulled my shoulder about and tied up my knee so tightly I couldn't walk! Where's Pipkin?"

"There he is!" said Patter – and sure enough there came Pipkin limping up the street looking very dusty and sorry for himself!

"You've bandaged the wrong pixie!" said Patter to the surprised doctor. "Oh my, oh my – he's bandaged the wrong pixie!

Patter began to laugh – and then Peri began – and when poor Pipkin limped up to the front door he could not *imagine* what was the matter with them!

"How unkind of you to laugh at me when I'm hurt," said poor Pipkin.

"Bandage this pixie, doctor," said Patter. But Dr Longbeard shook his head.

"No," he said. "I'm not bandaging any more pixies today. Goodbye!" And off he went.

So Patter took off Peri's bandages and

put them on Pipkin, who was very proud of them. And now he is sitting up in bed, hugging a hot-water bottle and drinking hot milk and feeling very happy indeed. What a muddle, wasn't it?

Silly Little Goofy

There was once a small pixie called Goofy who really did do silly things! He was always making tea without putting tea into the teapot and putting salt on his stewed apples instead of sugar. You really couldn't help laughing at him!

Have you heard how he tried to mend Hoho's motor hooter? You haven't? Well, I really must tell you and give you a good laugh.

Hoho had a large green-and-yellow car, and it had a fine hooter that went "pip-pip-pip" very loudly whenever he pressed it. He pressed it quite a lot, because the High Street in Goofy's village was always crowded with pixies, fairies and brownies doing their shopping.

But one day when Hoho pressed his fine hooter, it didn't make a sound. Not a pip came out of it, not a squeak. It was very sad. Hoho had to drive very slowly and carefully indeed, because he couldn't hoot people out of his way.

Goofy was almost run over, and he stopped and glared at Hoho. "I'm sorry, Goofy," said Hoho. "But my hooter has lost its pip. It just won't pip-pip any more. Listen!"

He pressed the hooter hard but no sound came out. Goofy pressed it too. "I think I can mend it for you, Hoho," he said.

"I'd rather you didn't, thank you," said Hoho, very quickly, for he knew

that Goofy often did very silly things. "Now, hurry on your way, Goofy. I'm going into this shop to buy myself a new pair of socks."

Hoho hopped out of his car and went into the shop. Goofy stood and stared after him. He felt sure he could put Hoho's hooter right, and he did so want to try.

"If the pip-pip has gone I could easily put it back again," thought Goofy. "I could buy an orange and put the pips inside the hooter – then it would be full of pips again and Hoho would be so pleased!"

Goofy waited till Hoho was safely inside the sock shop, and then he ran across the road to the fruit shop. He bought the largest orange he could see, and went back to the car. He got into it and peeled the orange. Goofy was not at all a tidy person and he scattered the peel all over the floor of Hoho's neat car.

Next Goofy got out his pocket-knife and made a small hole in the rubber part of the hooter. Then, one by one, he dropped the sticky orange-

pips inside. It was rather fun putting them in.

"I feel as if I am posting pips in a letterbox!" said Goofy. "There! That's the last pip. Goodness – I must have put about twelve into the hooter. It ought to say pip-pip very loudly indeed now!"

He pressed the hooter, expecting it to pip-pip as loudly as could be. But it didn't make a sound. Not the tiniest squeak came out of it at all!

Goofy was dreadfully disappointed. He stared at the hooter in dismay. Why wouldn't it pip-pip when he had put so many nice new pips inside?

"Perhaps it doesn't like orange-pips," said Goofy at last. "Perhaps it would rather have apple-pips. Yes – I feel sure it would rather have apple-pips."

So he went and bought an enormous ripe red apple. He sat in Hoho's car and ate it. It was most delicious. There were plenty of brown pips in the core. Goofy carefully saved them all.

"I'd better take out the orange-pips before I put in the apple-pips," thought Goofy. But it was very difficult to squeeze out the orange-pips. They just wouldn't come.

"Well, I'll put in the apple-pips on top of the other pips," thought Goofy. "I don't expect the hooter will mind."

Into the hooter went all the brown apple-pips too! And then Goofy pressed the hooter again, expecting it to shout "pip-pip-pip" very loudly indeed.

But no – not a single pip-pip came out of it! Goofy was upset. He began to wonder what Hoho would say when he came out of the sock shop. Perhaps he wouldn't be very pleased. Goofy decided he would go home.

Just as he had got out of the car, Hoho came along with the shopkeeper.

"If you'll let me unscrew your hooter and give it to my son to mend, I'm sure he can soon put it right for you," said the shopkeeper. So Hoho got the screwdriver and began to unscrew the hooter from the side of the windscreen. But as soon as he had got it off, he looked very puzzled.

"Listen!" he said to the shopkeeper. "This hooter rattles!" He shook it – and sure enough it rattled, which was not at all surprising considering what a lot of pips there were inside!

Hoho was most puzzled, and so was the shopkeeper. They both looked at the hooter in astonishment. Then Hoho saw the little hole in the rubber of the hooter and was even more surprised.

"Look at that hole," he said. "What made that, I wonder?"

"Moths, do you think?" said the shopkeeper.

"Of course not. Moths don't eat rubber, silly," said Hoho. He shook the hooter again, and then he made the hole a little bit bigger – and out came about twelve big orange-pips and eight large apple-pips! Goodness gracious, how Hoho stared!

"Who's been putting pips into my hooter?" he roared. "Who's been silly enough to think that pips in a hooter would mend it? Who ..."

And then he caught sight of Goofy

creeping away down the road, looking very red indeed. Hoho guessed at once that Goofy had been fiddling about with his hooter, and he gave an angry shout. He rushed after Goofy, took hold of his collar – and put all the orange-and apple-pips down poor Goofy's neck! You should have heard Goofy howl!

"That's right," said Hoho fiercely. "Run down the road squealing and squeaking like a hooter! Didn't I tell you not to touch my hooter? You wait till I see you next time, and I'll bump you right over in the road with my car!"

And Goofy is so afraid that he will, that he hasn't dared to go shopping for three days. Poor Goofy!

The Pixies
Make a Pie

Once upon a time the three pixies made a fine blackberry-and-apple pie. Peri picked the blackberries, Patter made the pastry top, and Pipkin put it in the oven to cook. It really was a lovely pie.

Now, when it was cooked and set on the windowsill to cool, the three pixies all had the same idea. But they didn't say a word to each other.

"That pie would be delicious with cream!" thought Peri.

"That pie would taste fine with cream!" thought Patter.

"That pie just wants good rich cream!" thought Pipkin.

But they didn't say this – because they all thought they would like to slip off to the dairy and get the cream as a surprise for the others!

Peri put on his hat and went to the milkman round the corner. He was a new milkman and he was pleased to see a customer coming to buy something.

"Good morning!" said Peri. "I've come to buy some cream. I've got a fine blackberry pie at home. My, you should see it! I thought a jug of cream would go with it very nicely indeed."

"Just the thing!" said the milkman, and he took the jug Peri had brought

with him. He dipped it into his big bowl of cream and filled it.

"Thank you," said Peri. "My word! Won't it be fine eating blackberry pie and cream! Please put it down on my bill, Mr Milkman."

"Where do you live?" asked the new milkman.

"I live in the little yellow cottage round the corner, the one with honeysuckle all over it," said Peri. "Goodbye, and thank you."

The milkman took out his book and wrote down Peri's address. "Pixie, yellow honeysuckle cottage – one jug of cream."

Peri went home, crept in at the side gate, and hid the cream on the top shelf of the larder. It was to be a surprise for the others. How pleased he was!

Now, in about half an hour, when the others were having a sleep in the garden, Patter thought *he* would go and get some cream for the pie. He didn't know about Peri's jug up on the top shelf of the larder.

He slipped out of the front door and took his jug to the dairy. The milkman was reading a paper behind the counter.

He was quite surprised to see a pixie again. He thought it was the same one he had seen a little while before.

"Good morning!" said Patter, grinning all over his jolly face. "I've got a fine blackberry pie at home, and I thought it would be nice to get some cream for it."

"You told me that before," said the milkman.

"Indeed I didn't!" said Patter, surprised.

"Indeed you did!" said the milkman.

"I tell you I didn't," said Patter, annoyed.

"I tell you you did," said the milkman, also annoyed. "But you can have some more cream if you want to."

"I *will* have some cream," said Patter, "but it's the first I've had today."

The milkman snorted rather rudely, took Patter's jug and dipped it into the bowl of cream.

"Thank you," said Patter. "Please put it on the bill. I live at the yellow cottage round the corner, the one with honeysuckle all over it."

"I know that already," said the milkman, taking down his book. "I don't forget things, even if *you* do!"

"I don't know what you mean," said Patter. He was beginning to think that the milkman was quite mad. "Good morning!"

He went home and put the cream in the china cupboard so that the others wouldn't see it. Then, grinning to think of the fine surprise he had for them, he slipped out into the garden, sat down in his chair and fell asleep.

Well, it wasn't long before Pipkin woke up and saw the others asleep. And into his head came the thought that it would really be a good time to slip off now, whilst the others slept, and get some cream for the blackberry pie.

He didn't know, of course, that there was already a jug of cream in the larder and one in the china cupboard!

So he crept quietly out of the garden and ran round the corner to the dairy.

"Good morning!" he said, going in. The milkman looked up.

"Oh, hello! So you're back again!" he said.

"I haven't been before," said

Pipkin, surprised.

"Oh no, oh no, oh dear me, no!" said the milkman. "I suppose you haven't got a blackberry pie at home, have you?"

"Well, yes, I have," said Pipkin, more surprised than ever.

"And I suppose you think you'll have a jug of cream to eat with your fine pie," said the milkman.

"Yes, I did think that," said Pipkin, holding out his jug.

"Well, all I can say is that you'll make yourself sick with all this cream," said the milkman, dipping his jug into the bowl of cream.

"You are a rude man," said Pipkin, feeling most annoyed.

"And you are a greedy pixie," said the milkman, handing Pipkin the jug.

Pipkin glared at the milkman. "Please put it on the bill," he said.

"Yes, I know that bit too," said the milkman, taking down his book. "And I suppose you still live at the yellow cottage round the corner?"

"Yes – but how did you know that?" asked Pipkin, astonished.

"And it's still got honeysuckle growing all over it?" said the milkman, writing in his book.

"Yes, it has," said Pipkin, thinking that the milkman must be a very peculiar man to know so much about a new customer.

"Right," said the milkman. "Well, if you come along again for a jug of cream today, don't bother to tell me it's for a blackberry pie. I shall know all right."

Pipkin went home, puzzled and cross. What a strange way for a milkman to behave!

He put his jug of cream under a bowl on the dresser, to hide it. He wanted it to be a surprise for the others.

Now, when suppertime came, the blackberry pie was put in the middle of the table. It did look nice.

Peri looked at it. "What that pie wants is a jug of cream to go with it," he said.

"It certainly does!" said Patter, thinking of the cream he had put in the china cupboard.

"Just the thing!" said Pipkin, thinking of his cream on the dresser.

They all grinned secretly to themselves.

Peri went to the larder and got his cream.
Patter went to the china cupboard and got
his. Pipkin went to the bowl and got his.
And they all went to the table at the same
moment and put their cream down on it!

"*Here's* the cream!" said Peri, Patter,
and Pipkin, all together. And then they
stared at each other's jugs in amazement.

"You got some too!" said Peri to
the others.

"And so did you!" said Patter.

"We all did!" said Pipkin. And then

they began to laugh and laugh and laugh.

"Three jugs of cream for one blackberry pie!" said Peri.

"Now I know why the milkman was so surprised when I went to get my jug of cream," said Patter.

"And I know why he was so rude when I went to get mine!" said Pipkin.

"He thought we were just one and the same pixie, keeping on walking in and telling him about our blackberry pie!" giggled Patter. "Oh, how funny!"

"Let's take him a piece of our pie with some sugar and cream for a treat, just to show him we are three pixies, not one!" said Peri.

So Peri cut a big piece of pie and piled juicy blackberries and apples all over the crust. Patter picked up the sugar basin. Pipkin poured some cream into a little blue jug and carried that. Then they all set off to the dairy.

First Peri went in with the plate of pie. The milkman looked rather alarmed. He had had enough of pixies that day.

"I've brought you a bit of our pie," said Peri, and put it down on the counter.

Then Patter came in with the sugar basin. "Help yourself to sugar," he said.

The milkman stared at him as if he couldn't believe his eyes. Two pixies, just exactly the same!

And then in came Pipkin with the little blue jug of cream.

"Pour a little cream over it and see how good the pie tastes," he said, with a large grin all over his face.

The milkman tried to speak but he couldn't. So that was the explanation – there were three pixies, not one – and they had each been to ask for cream. Oh

dear! Oh dear! He had been so rude.

"Don't worry," said Peri kindly. "Just eat the pie and enjoy it. We thought we'd come and show you we were three, not one. Good evening!"

The three pixies went home, sat down and ate that blackberry pie all up. They finished all the cream too, except a little they left for breakfast, to have with their porridge. My goodness, no wonder they are getting fat! I wish I'd had some of that pie, too, don't you?

The Three Pixies
up a Tree!

Once upon a time the three pixies, Peri, Patter and Pipkin, went for a long walk. They went over Bumble-Bee Hill and over Bumble-Bee Common and into Hello Wood.

"I'd like to climb a tree," said Peri, stopping at a tall chestnut.

"So would I!" said Patter, and he began to climb a sycamore.

"Here I go!" said Pipkin, and he shot up to the top of a young beech as fast as his legs would take him.

It was fun at the tops of the trees. Peri could see a long way. He could see the town in the blue distance, and he could even see the church bell shining in its tower.

Patter poked his head out at the top of his tree and saw Pipkin and Peri at the tops of theirs. That made him laugh. It was funny to see a pixie's head sticking

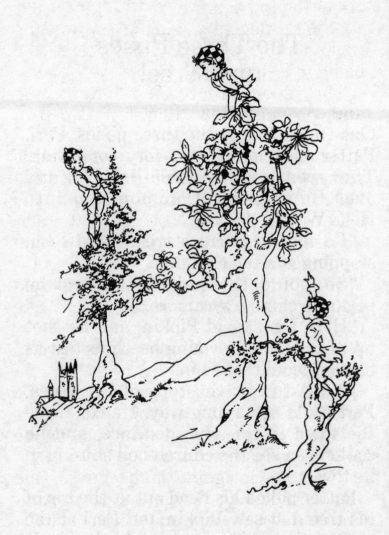

90

out of the top of a tree!

"This is lovely," said Patter, and he rocked his tree to and fro. "It's like being in a ship on the sea!"

They stayed there for a long time – and, do you know, Peri fell asleep in his tree!

He was sitting in a very comfortable place, with a broad branch behind his back, and he couldn't possibly fall. His eyes closed, he snored very gently, and no matter what the others called to him, he didn't answer!

"Peri! Peri! It's time to go home," said Patter. "Have you gone to sleep? Wake up, you silly pixie!"

There was no answer. Then Pipkin called to him:

"Peri! Don't be silly, pretending to be asleep! It's time to go home."

But Peri really was asleep, so he didn't answer a word.

"Patter, I'm going home now," said Pipkin suddenly. "I want to call at Aunt Caroline's on the way, so I'd better start."

He slipped down his tree and ran off to his aunt's. Patter stayed a little while longer, then he thought he would go, too, because it looked like rain.

"I can shelter in the woodman's hut if it does rain," he thought, and he climbed quickly down the tree. "Peri can stay in his tree if he wants to – but I'm not waiting for him." He shouted up to Peri, "Goodbye, Peri! I'm going! Come home when you're ready!"

Off he went, but it did pour with rain, so before he had gone very far he was soaked through. He ran to the woodman's hut and sheltered there.

The rain woke Peri at the top of his tree. The big raindrops splashed down on his face, and he dreamed that somebody was watering him!

"Don't water me, please!" he said. "Don't water me! I'm not a flower!"

But still the rain pattered down, and at last he awoke.

"Oh!" he said, astonished. "Where am I? What's all this water doing?"

He soon remembered that he was at the top of a tree, and he began to climb down out of the rain. But halfway down he got stuck. He couldn't get up and he

couldn't get down. He was just stuck there, very frightened.

"Patter!" he shouted. "Pipkin! Come and help me! I'm stuck in this tree, and I can't get down! Help! Help!"

But Patter and Pipkin were not there to hear him. Patter was sheltering in the woodman's hut and Pipkin was at his Aunt Caroline's, eating chocolate cake as fast as he could.

"Oooh!" yelled poor Peri. "The rain's wetting me! It's trickling through the leaves and going down my neck! Ooh!

Help! Help!"

Now, going through the wood was little Mr Fussy, under his big red umbrella. He was most astonished to hear a voice calling from somewhere. He put down his umbrella and listened.

"Help!" yelled Peri. "Help me, please!"

"Who wants help, and where shall I find you?" called Mr Fussy, looking round him in astonishment.

"I'm up in the chestnut tree!" yelled Peri. "Fetch a ladder! I can't get down! Quick, before I fall!"

Mr Fussy looked up in the chestnut tree and saw Peri there, looking quite pale.

"My goodness!" he said. "How did you get there?"

"How do you suppose I got here?" shouted Peri, quite cross. "Do you think I flew here, or got up the tree on roller-skates? Please fetch a ladder quickly!"

"All right, all right," said Mr Fussy, and he put up his umbrella again and hurried off to get a ladder. He knew where there was one – in the yard belonging to Mr Brick the builder. He got there, found the long ladder, and began to carry it back to the wood. He left his umbrella at Mr Brick's because it had stopped raining by now.

Now Patter, who had been sheltering in the woodman's hut, left it when the rain stopped. And he met Mr Fussy coming along, bent double under his ladder.

"Hello!" said Patter, astonished. "Where are you taking that to?"

Mr Fussy looked up, and when he saw Patter he couldn't believe his eyes. He thought he was Peri, you see, for all the pixies were as alike as peas in a pod.

"So you got down the tree?" he said.
"Of course I did!" said Patter, surprised. "What do you mean?"

"Well, why did you tell me you couldn't get down?" shouted Mr Fussy angrily. "I've been all the way back to get Mr Brick's ladder to get you down."

"But I didn't tell you I couldn't get down," said Patter. "You're making a mistake."

Mr Fussy gave a snort and ran at Patter with the ladder. Patter skipped off home as fast as he could, thinking

that Mr Fussy must be quite mad.

Mr Fussy took the ladder back to the yard, picked up his umbrella, and returned to the wood, for he had to pass through it on his way home. And no sooner did he get to that big chestnut tree than he heard Peri's voice as before:

"Oh, help! Help! Why doesn't somebody help me?"

Mr Fussy stopped in amazement. "Why, I've just seen you running off at top speed – and here you are up the tree again!" he said. "What do you want to go and climb the tree again for, when you couldn't get down last time? You are a very foolish creature."

"Oh, don't waste time talking!" begged Peri. "I'm very wet – and cold – and frightened – and unhappy. Oh, I thought you'd gone to get a ladder! Oh, dear Mr Fussy, do go quickly and get a ladder to help me! Can't you see how I've torn my coat on the branch? I shall fall soon, I know I shall!"

Mr Fussy thought it was all most peculiar, but as he really couldn't bear to see anyone stuck so uncomfortably up in a tree, he ran back to Mr Brick's yard again and got the ladder.

And as he carried it back to the wood, who should he meet this time but Pipkin, coming out of his Aunt Caroline's house, very pleased with himself because he had had three slices of chocolate cake. Mr Fussy put down the ladder and glared at Pipkin in a rage. He thought Pipkin was Peri, of course!

"What are you glaring at me like that

for?" asked Pipkin, offended. "Is my hat crooked? Or did I tread on your toe in a dream last night? What's the matter?"

"The matter is," said Mr Fussy in a trembling voice, "the matter is, that here I've been twice to get this ladder to get you down the tree – and I meet you walking along looking as cheeky as a jackdaw. You said you couldn't get down that tree."

"Oh no, I didn't," said Pipkin. "I got down quite easily. What are you talking about?"

"I'll teach you to trick me!" yelled Mr Fussy, and he ran so suddenly at Pipkin that the pixie was knocked over flat. Pipkin was quite scared, and he jumped up and ran home as fast as he could, wondering what made Mr Fussy behave in such a peculiar manner.

Mr Fussy took back the ladder, and then, grumbling and muttering, went back to the wood on his way home. And, of course, he soon heard Peri's anxious voice again:

"Is that you? Have you come back with the ladder? Mr Fussy, don't say you haven't brought the ladder!"

"What!" cried Mr Fussy, in the greatest astonishment. "Are you trying to play that trick on me again? Twice I've gone to get the ladder, and twice I've met you walking to meet me! And no sooner do I turn my back to take back the ladder than you spring up the tree again and wait for me to come by! But I'm not doing anything *this* time – no – all I'm going to do is to get you down the tree and spank you well."

And with that Mr Fussy picked up the old conkers that lay beneath the chestnut tree and began to throw them at poor Peri. *Bang! Bang! Smack! Bang!* They hit Peri on the nose and the chest and the knee and the ear. He yelled and tried to scramble back up the tree.

But the branch broke – and down he slid to the ground with a bump that shook all the breath out of his body.

And just as Mr Fussy was going to spank him well, who should come running up but Patter and Pipkin! They had come to look for Peri as he had been such a long time coming home.

"Leave him alone, leave him alone!" cried Patter, running to stop Mr Fussy from spanking Peri with his red umbrella.

"You bad fellow!" shouted Pipkin.

Mr Fussy looked up. He saw a pixie on the ground. He saw another on one side of him, and a third on the other – and they all looked exactly alike!

"It's a bad dream!" he shouted. "One pixie has turned into three! Help! Help! Help!"

And he tore off at top speed, leaving the three pixies staring after him in astonishment.

Poor Mr Fussy! He did his best, didn't he! He always runs away when he sees a pixie now – and really, I'm not the slightest bit surprised.

The Runaway Apples

Once upon a time Chuckle and Ho-Ho had a great many apples on their apple-tree. They were lovely apples, red and round, and as sweet as sugar.

"What shall we do with so many?" said Ho-Ho. "We can't eat more than three a day each, and we have already filled our apple-room."

"We must sell them," said Chuckle. "But who will buy them?" said Ho-Ho. "Everyone in our village has apples this year. It is a good apple year. No one will buy from us."

"I know someone who has no apples!" said Chuckle. "What about old Dame Cinders, up on the hill? She hasn't any fruit trees in her garden at all!"

"We'll send Trotter up the hill with a note to ask Dame Cinders if she'd like to buy our apples," said Ho-Ho, pleased. So they called Trotter, their dog, and he came trotting up, a neat little dog with sharp eyes and a wagging tail. "Woof!" he said politely.

"Take this note to Dame Cinders, Trotter," said Ho-Ho, and he gave the note to the dog. Trotter took it in his mouth and ran off. Very soon he came back with the answer.

"Hurrah!" said Chuckle, when he had

read the note. "Dame Cinders will buy a large basketful! Isn't that good! You can take them today, Ho-Ho."

"*I* can take them!" cried Ho-Ho, in surprise. "Well, I like *that*, Chuckle! Indeed I shan't take them. We will take them together."

"But I have a great deal of work to do," said Chuckle, who hated walking up the long, steep hill to Dame Cinders' cottage.

"Well, if I take the apples, I get the money, that's all," said Ho-Ho, and he went to fetch the apples. But Chuckle did not mean to let Ho-Ho take all the money. Oh, no, indeed! He ran out and helped him get the apples too, and together the gnomes packed them into the biggest basket they had. Then off they set together up the hill.

Now when they got almost to the top Ho-Ho began to glare at Chuckle in a very angry manner.

"What's the matter?" said Chuckle. "You look as if you are going to burst! You are all red and angry, Ho-Ho."

"Will you please tell me why you are

making me take all the weight of this heavy basket?" said Ho-Ho in a fierce voice. "I am carrying nearly all the basket – you are not helping a bit."

"I *am*!" said Chuckle angrily.

"You're *not*!" said Ho-Ho crossly, and he gave the basket a jerk. "There! If you had been holding the basket firmly I couldn't have jerked it like that!"

"Oh, *I* can jerk it too!" said Chuckle at once, and he gave the basket a big jerk from his side – and dear me, the basket overturned, and out fell the apples, *plop, plop, plop, plop*, one after the other! Chuckle and Ho-Ho smacked each other – and then they cried out in alarm – for all the red, round apples were rolling merrily down the hill! *Jumpity-jump, plippitty-plop, hippetty-hop!* Off they went, rolling and jumping for all they were worth!

"Catch them quickly!" cried Ho-Ho, and the two gnomes rushed after them. But those apples had got a good start, and how they raced down that hill! They didn't stop till they got right to the bottom. The gnomes picked them up without a word and took the basket up the hill again. But this time they didn't jerk the basket at all. No – they held it tightly until they got to Dame Cinders' cottage!

But Dame Cinders didn't like the look of the apples at all! She peered down at them through her big spectacles and turned up her long nose.

"And what sort of apples are *these*?" she said. "Just look at them! They're all bruised and cut and scratched! What in the world have you been doing to them? Have you been playing football with them?"

106

"No, Dame Cinders," said Chuckle, going red. "They fell out of the basket and rolled down the hill."

"Well, will you please take them back and bring me some good ones," said the old woman, going indoors. "I am not going to buy apples you have played marbles with!"

The two gnomes went down the hill again. They gathered some more apples from the tree in their garden and placed them carefully in the basket. Then up the hill they went again. When they were nearly at the top who should come scampering after them but Trotter, their little dog!

"Go back home, Trotter!" said Ho-Ho sternly.

"No, let him stay," said Chuckle.

"If I say he is to go back, he must obey me," said Ho-Ho.

"And if I say he is to stay, he is to obey *me*!" said Chuckle.

"Go home, Trotter!" shouted Ho-Ho.

"Come here, Trotter, come here!" shouted Chuckle.

Poor Trotter! He ran back a few steps

and then he rushed up to Chuckle – then back he went again – and up he came once more, not knowing at all what to do!

"Go home!" yelled Ho-Ho in a temper.

"Come here!" yelled Chuckle in a rage.

And then suddenly Ho-Ho dipped his hand into the basket, took out an apple and threw it down the hill!

"Go after it, Trotter!" he called. "Take it home!"

The apple rolled down the hill and Trotter galloped after it. Chuckle was in such a temper that he too put his hand into the basket – but he didn't throw the apple down the hill – no, he threw it straight at Ho-Ho!

Plop! It hit Ho-Ho on the nose. And then, what an apple fight there was! *Plop! Plop!* went the apples as the two gnomes flung them hard at one another.

Whenever the apples reached the ground they went rolling down the hill again. Not until all the apples were gone did the two gnomes think how silly they had been. They looked at the empty basket. They looked down the hill – and

there, at the bottom, they saw little dog Trotter busily chewing all their nice red apples!

"Dame Cinders won't want to have those either," said Ho-Ho sadly. "Why did we quarrel, Chuckle? That's twice we have wasted our apples. Now we shall have to go all the way home again to pick some more apples and climb all the way up the hill again – for the third time!"

"We won't be so silly again," said Chuckle. So the two gnomes carried the empty basket down the hill, left the nibbled apples for the wasps to finish up, and picked some more from their tree. When they had finished they felt tired.

"We will have some lemonade before we climb that hill again," said Ho-Ho. So the two sat down and drank lemonade and ate ginger buns. Then they set off up the hill once more. They had locked Trotter indoors, so he didn't come with them. The gnomes were most polite and kind to one another. They did not mean to quarrel again!

They got to the top of the hill. They

went up the garden path to the cottage and knocked at the door. Dame Cinders opened it.

"What do you want?" she said. "We've brought you the apples," said Ho-Ho politely. "They are the best we have. Not one is bruised or scratched. The basketful is fifty pence."

"Dear me, they certainly look good," said Dame Cinders. "But I don't want any apples now. Mister Chuffle has

111

just been along and given me a tubful for nothing. You are too late, Ho-Ho and Chuckle."

The two gnomes went sadly down the hill.

"If we hadn't been so silly, we would have got there first," said Chuckle. "It will teach us not to quarrel, Ho-Ho."

It did. They haven't quarrelled once since that day – but, oh dear, how tired they got of eating apple pudding! Poor Ho-Ho and Chuckle!

The Three Pixies
at the Station

Once it happened that Peri went away to spend a night at his Aunt Keziah's. The other pixies saw him off in the bus that started from the railway station, and waved goodbye to him.

"It will seem funny without Peri tonight," said Patter to Pipkin, as they walked back home. "Oh, look – there's the postman. I wonder if he has any letters for us."

The postman had a letter for Pipkin. He opened and read it.

"Dear me!" he said to Patter. "I must go to town tomorrow to be fitted for my new suit. This letter says it is almost ready for me. I shall have to catch the ten o'clock train."

"Peri's bus comes back just after ten o'clock," said Patter. "I will see you off first, Pipkin, then meet Peri off the bus."

But when tomorrow morning came,

Pipkin was very late for the train. He lost his purse and took such a long time hunting for it that Patter was quite sure he would miss the train.

"Pipkin! Here's my purse," said Patter at last. "Do go. I am sure you will miss the train. Run fast, Pipkin, for goodness' sake!"

Pipkin took the purse, clapped his hat on his head, and shouted goodbye to Patter.

"I'll walk slowly along to the bus stop

and meet Peri," shouted Patter. "I can't run all the way to the station to see you off, Pipkin."

So Pipkin raced off by himself, puffing and panting, and Patter put on his hat and walked slowly along to the bus stop by the station.

Pipkin soon got to the station. The train was just coming in. "Hi! Hi! I'm catching that train!" yelled Pipkin to the station-master. "Don't let it go without me! Hi! Hi!"

"You've got to get your ticket," said the station-master, trying to stop Pipkin from jumping into the train.

"Haven't time!" panted Pipkin, trying to push the station-master out of the way.

"You just go and get your ticket!" ordered the station-master crossly.

"Can't, I tell you! I shall miss the train!" puffed Pipkin, trying to run round the station-master.

"You get your ticket or you won't travel by this train," shouted the station-master, trying to get hold of the pixie, who was dodging all round him.

Every one was watching and giggling.

The guard suddenly blew his whistle and waved his flag. The train gave a shriek and began to puff out of the station.

"I must get in. I must, I must!" shouted poor Pipkin, and he tried to dodge round the station-master again. He bumped right into him and got round him. He jumped into a carriage and slammed the door.

The station-master ran after him, shouting angrily, and tripped up. He sat down on the platform in surprise and watched the guard's van whizz past him. How angry he was!

"You wait till I catch you!" he yelled after the train. Pipkin leaned out of his window and waved to him, grinning all over his face.

The station-master got up and went grumbling along the platform, scowling – and who should come into the station at that very moment, to buy himself some chocolate, but Patter. He had come to meet Peri's bus and there was just time to buy some chocolate.

The station-master stopped and stared at Patter, who was exactly like Pipkin.

He stared so hard that Pipkin was cross.

Then the station-master stopped staring and glared instead. He made a furious noise deep down in his throat and said, "Did you jump out of the train? How did you get here?"

Patter was surprised. "Don't be silly," he said. "I got here on my legs."

"You must have jumped out of the train," said the station-master angrily. "You simply must! One minute you're waving goodbye – and the next you walk on my platform as bold as brass."

"I don't know what you are talking about," said Patter. "I just came to buy some chocolate. I really haven't got time to waste in talking to a silly fat person like you."

Now that was very rude of Patter, and it made the station-master go quite mad with rage. He took hold of Patter's collar and shook the surprised pixie so hard that two buttons burst and flew off on to the platform.

"Stop, stop!" cried Patter. "You've no right to do this to me."

"Well, you deserve it!" shouted the

station-master. "First you won't buy a ticket – then you dodge past me – and then I trip over – and you grin at me through the window. Now here you are walking on to the platform, being cheeky all over again."

Patter wriggled away and ran down the platform. He really felt quite frightened. The station-master ran after him. Patter ran over the railway bridge and down the other side. The station-master took a short cut over the rails and nearly caught Patter as he came down the steps. Patter turned at once and ran all the way up the steps again – and the station-master ran back over the railway and waited for him again. It was dreadful.

Well, nobody can run up and down steps all morning, and Patter was soon tired out. The station-master caught him and marched him off to the luggage office and locked him in. Patter was very sad. There was a little barred window and he could see out of it. He saw Peri's bus coming into the station yard – and there was Peri inside.

Peri got out, and looked round for Patter and Pipkin, whom he thought would be there to meet him. But they weren't. So he went along to the station platform to see if by any chance they were there, watching the trains.

Well, they weren't, of course – but the station-master was there, looking very pleased with himself because he had caught Patter. Peri went up to him and tapped him on the shoulder.

"Do you know if ..." began Peri, and then stopped in alarm at the sight of the station-master's face. First it went red and then purple.

"You again!" gurgled the angry station-master. "You again! First you go off in a train without a ticket – then you go running up and down the bridge steps for half an hour! And now, after I've locked you up in my luggage office, you come and tap me on the shoulder!"

"Don't be silly," said Peri. "I've just come off the bus."

"But – but – but stammered the poor station-master, "but – but ... you can't go off in the train – and then get locked up – and then come along saying you've arrived in the bus. You simply can't have come in the bus."

"How dare you say I'm telling fibs!" cried Peri in a rage. "Look – there's the bus-driver, come to buy a paper. Excuse me – this man says I didn't come by bus. Just tell him I did, will you?"

"You certainly did," said the bus-driver. "I remember giving you a ticket."

"Oh dear! I simply don't understand this," said the poor station-master, wiping his forehead with a large red handkerchief. "I must be having a bad dream, or something – with nothing but rude pixies in it."

"Well, good-day," said Peri, and walked off home, wondering why Pipkin and Patter hadn't come to meet him. He didn't know that Patter was a prisoner in the luggage office and that Pipkin had gone to town.

The station-master watched Peri walking down the station road. "Well, let's hope that's the last of him," he grumbled. "Going off on a train – and buying chocolate – and arriving in a bus. Never heard of such a thing. How can one person be in three places at once?"

He went to get something out of the luggage office. He unlocked the door – and there, sitting on a large trunk, looking very upset, was Patter.

The station-master stared at him as if he couldn't believe his eyes.

"Now just look here!" he said, beginning to be angry all over again. "I've

seen you walking down the road this very minute – and now here you are again, sitting in my luggage office! What do you mean by it?"

"Well, you put me here," said Patter. "You must be mad, I think."

Patter stood up. He watched for a chance to escape. He suddenly pushed the station-master right over, rushed out of the door, and locked it behind him.

"Now he's a prisoner, and he can't come after me," thought Patter, pleased. "I'll just rush home as fast as ever I can!"

So home he went, giggling every time he thought of the station-master shut in his own luggage office.

Well, the station-master yelled and howled, he banged on the door and hammered on it till all the porters were quite scared. At last one unlocked the door – and out sprang the station-master, purple in the face. He glared round, expecting to see the pixie again. But Patter and Peri were both at home, eating their dinner – and Pipkin was in the train, now coming home again.

The train pulled in at the platform – and out sprang Pipkin. The first thing he saw was the station-master. He grinned at him and held out his ticket. "I got it at the other end," he said. "So you needn't glare at me like that."

"You're b-b-b-back again!" stammered the alarmed station-master. "How do you manage to get about like this? And what do you mean by locking me into

124

the luggage office?"

"How could I, when I've just arrived by train!" said Pipkin with a grin. "But I'd *love* to lock you into the luggage office! I'll do it, if you like!"

That was too much for the station-master. "No, no, no!" he cried, and he ran off as fast as his legs would take him. "No, no! I've had enough of you this morning! I'm going home!"

And home he went, much to Pipkin's surprise. How he and Patter and Peri laughed when they met and told one another about the peculiar behaviour of the poor station-master.

As for the station-master himself, he still doesn't understand to this day how it was that one pixie could do so many things!

The Three Pixies
and the Cats

Peri, Patter and Pipkin were getting their dinner ready one day when Peri found that someone had been nibbling at the cheese.

"Hello!" he said, lifting up the dish. "Which of you two has been nibbling our cheese?"

"*I* haven't," said Patter, looking quite offended.

"And I wouldn't *dream* of doing such a thing!" said Pipkin.

"Well, then, it must be mice," said Peri, and he looked solemnly at the others. "Mice in the larder! This will never do, will it? We shan't have a thing left. Our bacon will go. Our cheese will be nibbled. Our bread will be eaten. We simply *must* get rid of those mice."

"There's only one way," said Patter.

"What's that?" asked the other two.

"Get a cat!" said Patter. "That's

what we must do."

"Right!" said Peri. "We'll look out for a good mouser. We'll let her sleep in the larder at night and then the mice will soon go."

"And so will the milk and the bacon and the fish!" said Pipkin. "No – we'll keep her in the kitchen. The mice will smell her out in the kitchen, and they'll scurry off. If they come into the kitchen she'll catch them."

Now that afternoon Peri went out to buy some chocolate. At the shop was a beautiful black cat with green eyes. She lay on the counter and blinked lazily at Peri.

He remembered the mice in the larder. "I say," he said, "is that cat a good mouser?"

"Splendid," said the shopkeeper.

"Will you sell her to me?" asked Peri. "No," said the man. "We're fond of her. But she's got some black kittens exactly like herself. You can have one of those for nothing, if you like, if you promise to give her a good home. We want to find homes for them now."

"Oh, thanks very much," said Peri, pleased. The man went into his room at the back, and came out with a basketful of fine black kittens. There were three of them, all with green eyes like their mother. Peri picked up one of them and it cuddled against him.

"I'll have this one," he said. "It's a darling. Thank you very much."

Peri went off with the kitten. He had to go to fetch his boots from the mender's, so he took the kitten with him. It was quite a long walk but the kitten didn't mind. It loved Peri.

Now not long after Peri had gone out, Patter yawned and stood up. "I'm going to get a paper," he said. "Then I'll go along and see Josie, Click and Bun in the Tree-House. Shan't be very long, Pipkin."

He went off down the street to the

shop. It was the same shop that sold chocolate to Peri. Patter walked in and grinned at the shopkeeper.

"A *Pixie Times*, please," he said.

"Here you are," said the man. "How's the kitten?"

Patter stared at him in surprise. "What did you say?" he asked.

"I said, 'How's the kitten?'" said the man.

"What kitten?" asked Patter.

"The kitten you took away," said the man.

"I didn't take any kitten away," said Patter.

"You did!" said the man. "You took it away under your coat."

"You're making a mistake," said Patter, "I have no use for a kitten!" And then he suddenly remembered the mice in the larder, and he looked at the shopkeeper. "Oh, I *could* do with a kitten!" he said. "Have you got one to spare?"

"What do you want another one for?" asked the man.

"I don't want another one," said Patter. "I haven't got one at all. But I do want one."

"Well, it's a bit funny, all this," said the man doubtfully. He went into his back room and brought out the basket with two black kittens in. "If you are really sure you didn't take one of my kittens just now, you can have one of these."

"Oh, thanks very much," said Patter, pleased, and he picked up the nearest kitten. It was such a little dear, and cuddled up to Patter at once.

Patter went off with it, thinking how glad the others would be to see the dear little kitten he had got. He set off to the Tree-House to visit Josie, Click and Bun, to show them the kitten.

Now Pipkin was bored at being left all alone in the house. He thought he would go and buy some sweets. So up he got and down the street he went. He came to the shop that sold chocolate, papers and sweets, and went inside.

"Some fruit drops, please," he said.

"These?" asked the shopkeeper, and gave him a packet. Then he looked closely at Pipkin. "How's the kitten getting on?" he asked.

"Don't be silly," said Pipkin. "I haven't got a kitten – or a puppy, or a duckling, or a lion-cub either!"

"That's not funny," said the shop-keeper, offended. "You took one of my kittens just now. I just wanted to know how the little thing was getting on."

"Well, how do I know what a kitten that I haven't got is doing?" said Pipkin. "What do you suppose it is doing? Drinking water from the goldfish bowl, or catching mice in my larder?"

Now as soon as Pipkin had said that, it reminded him of the real mice in his larder, and he stared eagerly at the shopkeeper. "I say – I would *like* a kitten very much," he said. "I suppose you haven't one to spare?"

"Look here," said the man, "am I going to spend all afternoon giving you my kittens – and then have you come back and say that you haven't got them?"

"You're mad," said Pipkin. "Quite mad. Do you suppose I'd ask you for a kitten if I'd got dozens?"

"Well, no, I suppose you wouldn't," said the shopkeeper. "But what do you *do* with them? You walk out of the shop with a kitten under your coat – and then you come back and say you don't know anything about them. It's all very mysterious to me."

"And to me, too," said Pipkin. "I really can't help thinking there's something wrong with you. But all the same, if you've got a kitten, I'd love to have it."

"Well, it's the last one I've got," said the shopkeeper, going into his back room. "And don't you dare to come back and ask for another."

He brought the last little black kitten out, and gave it to Pipkin. "Thanks very much," said Pipkin, pleased, for the little thing was a real pet, and snuggled up to him most lovingly. He went out of the shop with it. He thought he would go straight home and pop the kitten into the warm kitchen and wait for the others to come home so that they might have a surprise.

He opened the kitchen door and put the kitten there. Then he went upstairs to wash. As soon as he had gone upstairs, Patter came home with his

kitten. He popped it into the kitchen too,
and shut the door so that it couldn't get
out. Then he went to hang his things up
in the hall. As he was doing that, Peri
came home.

Peri brushed past him and went to
the kitchen. He popped his kitten in too,
thinking that it would be a marvellous
surprise for the others when they went
into the kitchen for tea.

"Patter! Pipkin! Come along and see
the surprise I've got for you!" cried Peri.
The others hurried to him and they all
went to the kitchen.

They opened the door – and there in
the middle of the floor were three black
kittens all playing happily together.

Now this was a great shock to all the
pixies, for they each knew they had only
put *one* kitten into the kitchen – and in
some extraordinary way that one kitten
seemed to have turned into three! All
the pixies stared in amazement.

Then they rubbed their eyes and
looked once again at the three black
kittens, all exactly alike, with their little
tails and bright green eyes.

"My eyes have gone wrong," said Peri. "I'm seeing three instead of one."

"So am I," said Patter.

"And I am too," said Pipkin. "This is dreadful. We shall have to wear glasses. To think that my kitten has changed into three!"

"*My* kitten, you mean!" said Patter in surprise.

"No, *mine*!" said Peri in amazement. "I brought the kitten home – and I can't imagine why it's turned into three."

The kittens ran to the pixies. One went to Peri, one to Pipkin, and one to Patter. The pixies stared at each other. "There must be *three* kittens really, after all!" said Peri. "But where did they all come from?"

"I got one from the shopkeeper," said Patter.

"And I got one from him too," said Pipkin.

"Well, so did I," said Peri. "The man must have been most surprised!"

"He was!" said Patter and Pipkin. "Gracious – what are we to do now? Shall we take two kittens back?"

"No – the man will think we are quite, quite mad if we go back again and take the kittens with us!" said Peri. "We'll have to keep them all!"

So they did – and if ever you visit the three pixies, you are sure to see three big black cats with green eyes sitting on the sofa – and you'll know how it is that there are three of them.

And, of course, there are *no* mice in the larder now!

Big-Hands
and Nobbly

Once upon a time Nobbly the goblin quarrelled with Big-Hands the gnome. They lived next door to one another and had always been good friends until this quarrel.

It was a very silly quarrel, really. It happened that Tip-Tap the butcher had called at Nobbly's with his meat, and Nobbly was out. So the butcher had left it on the windowsill – and when Nobbly came home he saw Big-Hands' cat licking the meat!

He rushed into Big-Hands' cottage in a furious rage.

"That cat of yours has licked my meat!" he cried. "Smack it, Big-Hands, smack it!"

"Certainly not," said Big-Hands, who was very fond of his cat. "How can you expect a cat not to lick meat if it is left on a window sill. You should go and scold the butcher for doing such a foolish thing. Why, any other cat but mine would have stolen the meat and taken it away to eat it! I think my cat should be praised, not punished for only just licking the meat. It must very badly have wanted to steal it altogether!"

Just at that moment the cat came in, licking its lips. Nobbly flew at it, and gave it a hard smack, so that it mewed in dismay and fled to a corner.

Big-Hands was very angry. He rushed at Nobbly and shook him – but Nobbly was a bony person to shake. He had great bony feet and long skinny arms

and a nobbly head. Big-Hands soon let him go – and then Nobbly fled to his cottage crying, "I'll pay you back for this, so I will!"

And he did too. He really was very naughty indeed. He threw all his rubbish over the wall into Big-Hands' garden. He lit his bonfire when the wind was blowing towards Big-Hands' cottage, so the poor gnome had his kitchen filled with smoke all day long. And he put his radio on very loudly indeed when he knew that Big-Hands was having his afternoon nap!

This made the gnome very angry. He ran up the path to Nobbly's front door and banged on the knocker. Nobbly wouldn't open the door, so Big-Hands stood on the doorstep and yelled at him.

"I'm going to punish you for all these unkind things! Yes, you look out, Nobbly! You'll be sorry for yourself, you will! I'll just show you what I can do! Grrrrrrrr!"

Big-Hands sounded so very fierce that Nobbly really felt rather frightened. Big-Hands did not usually lose his temper, for he was a good-natured fellow, but when he did people knew about it.

Nobbly looked at Big-Hands going down the path, from behind the curtains. He saw him doubling up his big hands into fists, and shaking them, muttering angrily all the time.

"Oooh!" thought Nobbly. "I'd better be careful. There's really no knowing what he might do!"

So that day Nobbly didn't throw any more rubbish over the wall, and didn't put his radio on. He went to bed early that night, read a book for a little while and then fell fast asleep.

When he woke up, the moon was shining outside his window. And, to Nobbly's great fright and horror, he suddenly saw what looked like two enormous hands sticking up at the end of his bed, looking for all the world as if they belonged to someone crouching behind at the foot of the bed, ready to pounce out!

Nobbly turned pale and shivered so much that even the bedsprings rattled.

"It's Big-Hands the gnome come to scare me!" he groaned to himself. "Oh my, oh my, look at those awful great

hands sticking up there, ready to come at me if I so much as speak a word."

Now, Nobbly had made a very great mistake. What he thought were hands were not hands at all – but simply his own great bony feet sticking up out of the bedclothes at the bottom of the bed! Nobbly was so bony that the bedclothes found it difficult to keep on him and were forever slipping off!

Nobbly lay and looked at his feet, thinking all the time that they were hands, and wondering what in the world he could do to frighten away Big-Hands, whom he thought was hiding at the end of the bed. Then suddenly the moon went behind a cloud and the room became dark. Nobbly decided to creep out of bed and light his candle.

He crept out, and went to the table by the wall where his candle stood. He lit it and then held it up to see Big-Hands – but, of course, there was no one at the end of the bed at all! No – not a sign of Big-Hands the gnome! It was most puzzling!

"He's gone!" said Nobbly, pleased. "Oh, what a fright he gave me, the horrid creature! What shall I do if he comes again tomorrow night? I shan't dare to go to bed! I shall go and complain to Constable Stick, the policeman."

So the next morning Nobbly went to the cottage where Constable Stick the policeman lived. He was just finishing his morning cup of cocoa, and he listened in surprise when Nobbly told him what he had seen the night before.

"Yes, I tell you," said Nobbly, all excited. "That nasty, unkind gnome came into my room in the middle of the night, hid himself at the end of my bed, and then, when I woke up, I saw his big hands sticking up ready to come at me! Think of that, now! Don't you think you ought to go and take Big-Hands to prison?"

"Well, no, I don't," said Constable Stick. "You see, you might have made a mistake, Nobbly. After all, you didn't see Big-Hands' face did you? It might have been somebody else."

"Pooh!" said Nobbly, scornfully. "It couldn't have been somebody else, Constable Stick! No one else in the village has such enormous hands as Big-Hands. I know they must have been his hands."

"Well, wait and see if he comes again," said Constable Stick. "I'll wait outside tonight, and if you give a call I'll come in and take Mr Big-Hands off to prison, if it really is him."

"But suppose he escapes before you come?" said Nobbly. "How shall I get hold of him? He is such a big fellow."

"Well," said Constable Stick, thinking hard, "you might take a piece of rope and make a loop in it, Nobbly. Then, if Big-Hands does come again and scares you by sticking up his great hands at the end of the bed, you just throw the loop of rope round them, draw it tight – and you'll have got him prisoner all ready for me to march off!"

"Ooh, that's a good idea!" said Nobbly, very pleased. He went home and got a piece of rope. He carefully made a loop in it and put it beside his bed, ready for the night. When his bedtime came he undressed, got into bed, and put the loop of rope under his pillow. Aha, Mr Big-Hands, just you wait!

He fell asleep – and woke again with a jump just after midnight. And dear me, bless us all, there were his great bony feet sticking up again in the moonlight looking like enormous hands!

"Oh, Big-Hands, it's you again, is it?" cried Nobbly, and he fished under the pillow for his loop of rope. In a flash he had it out and threw it neatly over what he thought were the hands at the foot of the bed – but of course they were his own feet! He pulled the loop tight, and then gave a scream.

"Oh, oh, let go of my feet, Big-Hands! Oh you wicked gnome, you've got my feet!"

As the rope pulled tighter and bound his feet together poor Nobbly rolled about in the bed. He thought he had got hold of Big-Hands with the rope, so he pulled and pulled – and the more he pulled the more tightly the rope cut into his nobbly feet!

"Ow! Ow! Help! Help!" yelled the goblin, and rolled off the bed with a bump. He tried to get up, but of course his feet were tied together and he fell over each time he tried. He was really dreadfully frightened.

"Constable Stick, Constable Stick, come and help me!" he called. "Big-Hands has got me by the feet and won't let go!"

Now Constable Stick had been hiding in the garden, as he promised – but he had fallen asleep. He woke up in a hurry when he heard such a yelling and

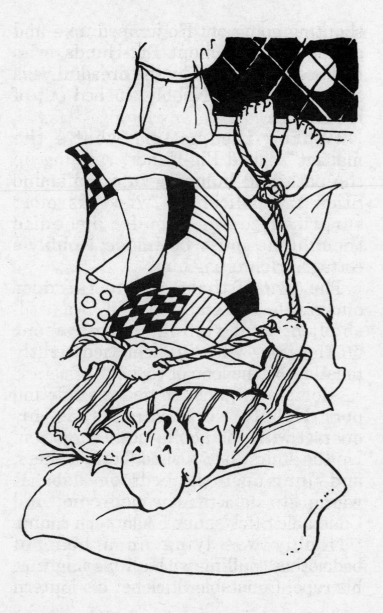

shouting going on. He jumped up – and at the same moment Big-Hands, who had been awakened by the dreadful yells and shouts from Nobbly, rushed out of his cottage.

"What's the matter, what's the matter?" called Big-Hands, running up the path and bumping into Constable Stick the policeman, who was most surprised to see him for he quite thought he must be inside Nobbly's cottage, frightening him!

The two of them opened the door and ran to the stairs. Nobbly was still shouting and yelling, rolling about on the floor with his feet tied tightly together by the loop of rope.

"Come on, quick, someone's hurting poor Nobbly!" cried Big-Hands, his quarrel with the goblin quite forgotten. Up the stairs they rushed, both of them, and flung open the bedroom door. It was quite dark in the bedroom, and Constable Stick shone his lantern round.

Nobbly was lying on a heap of bedclothes, pulling with all his might at his rope! Constable Stick set his lantern down on a table and helped Nobbly to get up.

"Someone's tied your feet together," said Big-Hands in astonishment, as he saw the loop of rope tied round the goblin's bony feet. "Whoever did that to you?"

"Why, wasn't it you?" said Nobbly in amazement, staring at Big-Hands.

"No, indeed it wasn't," answered Big-Hands at once. "I wouldn't do such a horrid thing! You ought to know that. Besides, Constable Stick the policeman will tell you I came rushing up the stairs with him – I wasn't in your bedroom at all. I do wonder who it was. Let's hunt around a bit and see if we can see any robber, shall we, Constable Stick?"

They untied poor Nobbly's feet and then, taking the lantern, they all hunted round the cottage – but, of course, there was no one there at all! They couldn't understand it.

"I'm so frightened!" wept Nobbly. "I can't make it out. Who is the person with great, enormous hands who keeps coming to frighten me? Oh dear Big-Hands, do please stay with me for the rest of the night and sleep here so that I shan't be alone. Then, if the person comes again, you will be able to scare him away for me. You are so brave."

"Very well," promised Big-Hands. So they said goodnight to Constable Stick, and off he went home. Big-Hands and Nobbly settled down to sleep in the bed

– it was rather a tight fit for two people – and soon nothing was to be heard but gentle snores from Nobbly and enormously loud ones from Big-Hands.

Well, Big-Hands suddenly gave such a tremendous snore that Nobbly woke up with a jump – and goodness me, there were his feet again, sticking up in the moonlight just like big hands coming to get him.

"Ooh! Oh!" yelled Nobbly, in a fright. "Wake up, Big-Hands! Look! Look!"

Big-Hands woke up with a jump and sat up in the moonlight. He saw at once what Nobbly was looking at – but he was wiser than the foolish goblin, and he knew that what Nobbly thought were hands, were really his own bony feet with the bedclothes off! He began to laugh. How he laughed!

He rolled over and over in the bed, dragging all the clothes from Nobbly and making him shiver with cold.

"Ho-ho-ho, ha-ha-ha, he-he-he!" yelled Big-Hands, the tears pouring down his cheeks. "Oh, Nobbly, you'll be the death of me, really you will! It's you own silly

big feet looking at you, not a robber's hands at all! Oh my, I've such a stitch in my side! What will you do next?"

Well, when Nobbly looked a little closer, and waggled his toes about to see if the hands really were his feet, he found that Big-Hands was right – and he went as red as a cooked beetroot! You should have seen him. He did feel so ashamed of himself. Whatever would Constable Stick say? And what would all the village say too when it heard the tale of how Nobbly had been scared of his own feet – and had even tied them up in a loop of rope, and rolled about the floor! Oh dear! What a dreadful silly he was, to be sure.

"Oh, Nobbly, you'll be the joke of the town tomorrow!" laughed Big-Hands, wiping the tears of laughter from his eyes.

"Big-Hands, don't tell anyone," said Nobbly, in a small voice. "Please be friends with me again – and don't tell anybody about this. I do hate to be laughed at."

"Well, you deserve to be," said Big-Hands. "You have been very unkind lately, Nobbly – smacking my cat, and throwing rubbish into my garden, and letting your bonfire smoke come into my kitchen, and playing your radio when I am trying to have a nap. You don't deserve any kindness from me. No – I think everyone must hear this funny story about you. It's such a joke!"

"Oh please, Big-Hands, I know I've been unkind and horrid," wept the goblin. "But I won't be again. I do want to be friends with you. You were so kind to stay with me tonight. I will buy your cat a nice fresh fish from the fish shop each day for a fortnight if you will forgive me, and promise not to tell anyone at all."

"Well, that's a kind thought of yours," said Big-Hands, who was always pleased when anyone was good to his cat. "I'll forgive you and be friends again, then, Nobbly. But you won't mind if I have a good laugh now and again, will you, when I think about tonight? For really it was very, very funny!"

So now the two are great friends once more, and Big-Hands' cat can't understand her good luck when she is given a fish each day by Nobbly the goblin!

And, sometimes, when Nobbly is a bit silly and does foolish things, Big-Hands looks at him with a twinkle in his eye, and begins to laugh. "Do you remember when you caught your own feet instead of a robber?" he chuckles. Then Nobbly goes red, and stops being silly. He does so hate to be reminded of the night when he thought his feet were hands!

Big-Hands and Nobbly

The Three Pixies
and Mr Tubby

Once upon a time, Mr Tubby came to live with his Aunt Amanda in the village where the three pixies lived.

Now Mr Tubby had a habit of walking along the street without looking where he was going, especially if he had his umbrella up. So he often bumped into people, and this made him very angry indeed.

It wasn't long before he bumped into one of the pixies because he took a walk down their street twice a day. It was Peri he bumped into first.

Peri was running to catch the bus. Peri always had to run to catch the bus because he could never start out in time. So he ran out of his front gate, turned into the street – and bumped straight into Mr Tubby!

Peri was running quite fast and Mr Tubby was big. So they had a wonderful

collision and quite knocked the breath out of each other.

"Now look here," said Mr Tubby in a rage, when he got back his breath. "Now look here! Now ..."

"Don't say it again," panted Peri. "I don't want to look. I want to catch the bus."

"Now look here!" began Mr Tubby again, waving his stick. "I won't have you rushing at me like that and bumping into me! I won't have it, I say! Why, I nearly bit my tongue in half when you banged into me."

"It's a pity you didn't," said Peri. "Then you wouldn't be able to talk so much. Let me pass, please. I want to catch my bus!"

Mr Tubby tried to catch him, but Peri slipped by and rushed for the bus. He only just caught it in time, and even then the driver had to wait for him.

Peri sat down, panting like a goldfish out of water.

Mr Tubby went on with his walk, muttering angrily to himself about pixies that had no manners. He went to the end of the street, up on to the common, and then turned back. And most unluckily he met Patter rushing home from the shopping, afraid that he would be late in cooking the lunch. Patter had so many parcels that he really couldn't see Mr Tubby.

So he bumped right into him. *Bang, crash!* Patter's parcels fell all over Mr Tubby, and two beautiful new-laid eggs broke on his head and slid down his neck.

"Oh, my eggs, my eggs!" groaned Patter. "You silly fellow, why didn't you look where you were going?"

Mr Tubby sat on the pavement and glared at Patter in a furious temper. "Good gracious, so it's you again!" he cried. "Do you spend your time bumping into people and knocking them over? Are you doing this on purpose?"

"I've never bumped into you before – or behind either," said Patter furiously, picking up his parcels.

"You story-teller!" shouted Mr Tubby. "You're the one that's telling stories," said Patter, and he marched off, his nose high in the air.

Mr Tubby picked himself up and went

home, telling himself all the dreadful things he would like to do to pixies that bumped into him.

Now, that afternoon Mr Tubby had to go out again to fetch some fish for his Aunt Amanda. It was raining, so he took his umbrella with him and put it up. He walked off with it held well in front of him and everyone had to skip out of his way or he would have walked into them.

Now Pipkin had to go out that afternoon, too. He had to fetch a book from the library, and he was in a hurry because that day the library closed at three o'clock. So he hurried along with his umbrella up, and peeped out now and then to make sure he wasn't going to run into anyone.

Round the corner came Mr Tubby, with his umbrella held in front of him – at exactly the same moment as Pipkin also came round the corner, with *his* umbrella in front of him too.

Crash! They ran into one another, and tore their umbrellas dreadfully! They fell down on the path and gasped for breath. Mr Tubby looked round his torn umbrella to see who it was that had collided with him like that – and lo and behold, there was Pipkin the pixie staring angrily at him out of his big eyes! His face was going red with rage!

"What! You again!" cried Mr Tubby, spluttering like a cat under water.

"What do you mean – me again?" said Pipkin crossly. "It's certainly me – but it

isn't me-again!"

"Do you wait round every corner for me?" yelled Mr Tubby.

"Shouldn't dream of it," said Pipkin. "You're being silly."

"Silly! Well, what about *you*?" said Mr Tubby, in a rage. "You bump into me every time you can – and knock me over – and now you've torn my umbrella."

"This is the first time I've knocked you over," said Pipkin. "And you knocked *me* over too – and tore *my* umbrella – but I don't go about saying that you bump into me every time you can."

"I've hurt my leg," said Mr Tubby, trying to get up. "Oh, you bad pixie, you've made me hurt my leg. It's bleeding."

So it was. "Well, you'd better come to my house and I'll bathe it for you," said Pipkin, who had a very kind heart. "Mind you, I don't think you deserve it – but I'll take you home and see to your leg."

So he helped Mr Tubby to his house and got him into the warm sitting-room. He put him on the sofa. Mr Tubby closed his eyes, for he really felt rather bad after having been knocked over three times in one day.

Pipkin called Patter and Peri. "I've got a silly man here who bumped into me and tore my umbrella," he said. "He's hurt his knee. You bring some warm water, Peri, and Patter, see if you can find a bandage."

Pipkin went back to Mr Tubby and rolled down his sock for him. Mr Tubby opened his eyes feebly. He saw Pipkin. Then he saw Patter bringing a roll of bandage – and then, oh, my goodness, he saw Peri bringing a bowl of hot water.

"You've gone into three!" he groaned, and shut his eyes again. "You've gone into three. I can't bear it."

"What does he mean?" whispered Pipkin. "Is he mad?"

"A bit, I should think," said Patter. He looked closely at Mr Tubby. "Oh, my! It's the man I bumped into this morning when I came home from shopping!"

"And it's the one I knocked over when I ran to catch my bus!" said Peri.

"And I knocked him over, too, when I ran round the corner to the library!"

said Pipkin. "He thought we were all the same pixie. Oh dear – no wonder he thought we were waiting round corners all day, ready to bump into him whenever he came along!"

"Mr whatever-your-name-is," said Peri, "it's most unfortunate, but we've all bumped into you today! We're really very sorry. We're not *one* pixie, we're three. Do forgive us!"

Mr Tubby opened his eyes again and was most relieved to hear what Peri said. He sat up, feeling better at once.

"My name's Tubby," he said. "I am pleased to meet you – even if I wasn't pleased to bump into you! Thank you for bandaging my leg so nicely. Dear me, how alike you are! What are your names?"

"I'm Peri, he's Patter, and he's Pipkin," said Peri. "Will you have a cup of tea? And we've some nice new ginger cakes too."

"Oh, thank you," said Mr Tubby, feeling very happy all of a sudden. "Yes – I'd love to stay and have tea. And you must come to tea with me tomorrow. We shall have some currant buns. My Aunt

Amanda makes them beautifully."

So they made friends – but poor Mr Tubby never knows which pixie is which, even though they go to tea with him once a week now.

Four Little Wheels

One of the oldest toys in Jack's room was a small motor-car. It had been there as long as the teddy bear had, and he had come when Jack was one year old.

There was a little tin man at the steering-wheel of the motor-car, and at night he drove his car round and round the room at top speed. Everyone got out of his way then, because it wasn't pleasant to be bumped into and yelled at and knocked over.

"Stop it, Tin Man," Teddy would say, crossly. "Look where you are going. That's twice you've run over the monkey's tail tonight."

"Well, he shouldn't leave it about so," said the tin man. "He should hold it up in the air or tie it round his waist or something. It's a most untidy tail."

The tin man wasn't always as cross as he sounded. He was a kind old fellow really, and the smaller toys could have a ride with him whenever they liked. He simply loved tearing along at top speed. It was the one joy of his life.

His car was looking rather old now. It had four tiny wheels, each with a little rubber tyre round it. The wheels had once been painted bright red, but now they were dented and didn't run very straight.

This made the motor-car wobble when it went round a corner. The tin man had tinkered about with them, but he couldn't mend them. He was always afraid one would come off.

There was another thing he was afraid of, too. He knew his car was old. He knew it looked dreadful. And he knew that old toys sooner or later were thrown away. They went into what Teddy called "The Land of the Dustbin." The toys hated to think about that.

When anyone was cross with the tin man they always said the same thing to him: "You'll soon be off to the Land of the Dustbin, you and your silly old car! It will serve you right for tearing round and round, running over tails, and knocking down dolls and skittles!"

Then the tin man would look at his old car and shiver a little. "Yes," he would think to himself, "I'm so afraid that Jack will soon want to send me away to that dreadful land. I have heard that tea-leaves live there too, and potato peel, and old newspapers, and broken glass. I don't want to go to the

Land of the Dustbin."

"*I* shan't go to the Land of the Dustbin," the old teddy bear would say proudly. "I have often heard Jack say that he will never part with me, never. I'm quite safe."

The tin man wished he was quite safe too. He was very upset one day when Jack's mother came into his room, looked into his toy cupboard and said, "Oh, Jack, what a lot of broken toys you have! You really must put some into the dustbin soon."

"Oh, Mum!" said Jack. "There's nothing I can spare, *really*!"

"Well, what about this awful old car?" said his mother, picking up the little motor-car, tin man and all. "Its wheels are almost off – the paint is gone. I'm sure you don't play with it any more. This is one of the first things that must go. Now, really, you must make a pile of your old broken toys and I'll pop them into the dustbin."

So Jack cleared out his toy cupboard and put some of the things into a pile. There was a very torn book. There was a broken brick box and some odd bricks. There was a game of snakes and ladders, broken in half, and a tiny rabbit without any head or tail. And, oh dear, there was the old motor-car with the little tin man.

"I don't like sending you away," said Jack to the little tin man. "But I suppose you are awfully old, and your car does look dreadful now. The wheels are loose, too."

The tin man stared miserably in front of him. When Jack had gone out of the nursery the toys crept out of the cupboard and went over to him.

"Bad luck, tin man," said the little furry dog. "We shall miss you."

"I do wish you weren't going," said the clockwork mouse. "But perhaps it won't be so bad in Dustbin Land after all."

"Don't talk about it," said the tin man in a choky sort of voice. "I'm sorry I ran over your tails, clockwork mouse and monkey. I'm sorry I knocked you down, furry dog. I'm sorry I frightened you so many times, tabby cat."

Nobody came to take the pile of

broken toys away that night. It stayed there in the corner of the nursery, the little toy motor-car on top, with the tin man looking miserably round at the toys playing on the carpet.

Suddenly outside the window there came a noise of high chattering. "It's the pixies," said the teddy bear, peeping out. "Going off to dance or something, I suppose."

There came a rapping at the window, and the monkey and the bear together managed to open it just a crack at the bottom. They didn't need to open it wide because the pixies were even smaller than the toys. A little pixie climbed in out of breath.

"I say!" she said in her little high voice, just like a bird's. "A dreadful thing has happened."

"What?" asked the toys, crowding round her.

"Well, my aunt, Flicker-Wings, is very ill and sent for me and my sister," said the pixie. "So we set off in our carriage, flying through the air, drawn by our big tiger-moth. But suddenly a bat swept down and snapped at our moth! We beat it off, but it has hurt one of the moth's wings so much that it can't fly. We simply *must* get to my aunt tonight, so we came here to ask if you've got anything that can fly, so that we can borrow it for our carriage – an aeroplane, say."

"No, we haven't," said the teddy bear. "But we could lend you the clockwork mouse if you liked, and he could drag your carriage over the ground. He can't fly in the air."

"But our carriage hasn't any wheels, silly," said the pixie. "It would go

bump, bump, bump all the time, and we shouldn't like it a bit."

"Couldn't we lend you some wheels to fix on it, then?" said the furry dog excitedly. "Train, how about you. Would you lend some?"

"No," said the train. "I'd go off the rails if I took off any wheels."

"Well, what about you, wagon?" said the bear, turning to the wagon nearby. But the pixie shook her head at once.

"Those wheels are much too big," she said. "We should only want very small ones."

A doleful voice called from the pile of rubbish. "You can have the four wheels off my motor-car, pixie. They are loose, so you can easily get them off, and they are the right size. I shall never want them again. I'm going to the Land of the Dustbin."

"Poor thing!" said the pixie at once. "I'm sorry for you. But it would be an awfully good deed if you could let us have your four little wheels. They are just the right size."

It wasn't long before the monkey and

the teddy bear had them off. The tin man stared at them sadly. "Well, I'm glad someone's going to be able to make use of them," he said, with a sigh, "I hope you'll manage to get them on your carriage all right."

"Oh, we shall use magic to do that," said the pixie. "It will be easy. We'll use some magic to make them a nice bright colour, too – bright blue, I think. My word, we *shall* have a fine carriage. Clockwork mouse, would you mind taking us to our aunt? Our carriage won't be very heavy to pull."

"Of course I'll take you," said the mouse. He went outside with the pixie. The teddy and the monkey went too, carrying the four old wheels with them.

"Hello!" said the pixie's sister in surprise. "What's all this?"

She was sitting in the carriage outside. It was on the grass. Nearby was a moth, stroking its hurt wing with its feelers. It was very sorry for itself.

"We'll leave you here till you feel better, moth," said the pixies. "We'll see our aunt, and then come back home this way, to see how you are. If you are no better you will have to squeeze into the carriage with us, and the clockwork mouse will drag us all home together, in our little carriage with wheels."

It was marvellous to see how quickly the four wheels were fitted on with magic. Just a wave of a wand and they were in their place under the carriage! Another wave of the wand and they turned a beautiful bright blue!

"As good as new!" said the clockwork mouse in surprise, putting himself in front of the carriage and letting the pixies harness him. "Well – off we go!"

And off they went, the little mouse running swiftly on his clockwork wheels through the night. The pixies had to wind him up three times, but that was all.

Their aunt was much better, and had got someone to look after her, so that was good. The pixies promised to come again tomorrow, and set off homewards, the little mouse going swiftly. "Go back to where we left the tiger-moth," said one of the pixies. "We must take him home if he isn't better."

But dear me, the moth was quite all right! He was flying round and round, waiting impatiently for the pixies to come back. He was feeling jealous of the clockwork mouse – it was *his* job, not a clockwork mouse's, to draw the pixies' carriage!

"I'm better!" he called, as the carriage came near. "Tell the mouse to go back home. And take off the wheels. They will be too heavy for me to pull along, for I am not so strong as the mouse."

"Oh, we are glad you are better again," said the pixies. They tapped each wheel with their wands and the wheels at once fell off. The clockwork mouse got out of the harness and the tiger-moth took his place.

"Will you take the wheels back to the tin man, and thank him very much for us?" said the pixies. The mouse said he would. He waved goodbye with his tail, put the wheels in a row down his back, and squeezed himself under a door. He went back to Jack's room and everyone was glad to see him.

"The pixies sent back the wheels,"

said the clockwork mouse. "Here they
are. They look quite new now, because
they aren't bent or dented any more –
and the pixies made them bright blue.
Won't the tin man's car look smart!"

The teddy bear put the four wheels

181

back on the car. The tin man was full of delight to see them looking so new and bright. "*What* a pity I shan't use them any more!" he said. "*What* a pity I'm going to Dustbin Land!"

The next day Jack's mother came to take the pile of rubbish – and how she stared when she saw the little motor-car on the top. "Look, Jack!" she said. "This isn't the old car I meant. This one looks new – see the dear little blue wheels? You can't put this into the dustbin. Put it back into your toy cupboard and when you find the one I meant take it down to the dustbin."

"I haven't got another one," said Jack, in surprise. "This must be the same one – with new wheels. I'd know my old tin man anywhere!"

You should have seen the tin man whizzing round and round the room that night, in his little motor-car with its bright blue wheels! He was as happy as he could be – and so were all the toys. Even when he ran over the monkey's tail he didn't get scolded, and they all joined in his joyful song:

"I'm not going off to
Dustbin Land!
Oh, isn't it grand,
yes, isn't it grand,
He's *not* going off to
Dustbin Land!"

The Pixies Say Goodbye

The great Lady Isabel Dumps had been staying in the village where the three pixies lived. Peri, Patter and Pipkin saw her in her fine carriage, and they thought she was very grand and very kind.

She opened two sales of work. She went to a play given by the village children, and was so pleased with the way they acted that she gave them a box of chocolates each. She visited all the old ladies and left each of them a warm red shawl and a packet of tea.

So, you see, she really was very sweet and kind, and everyone loved her.

She stayed for a month in the village, and then she said she must go back home.

"What a pity!" said Peri. "I would have liked her to stay longer. It is true that we have never spoken even a word to her, but still it's nice to have someone like Lady Isabel Dumps taking an interest in our village."

"There is going to be a band at the station to see her off," said Patter.

"The children are going to give her the biggest bunch of roses you ever saw," said Pipkin.

"The engine and the carriages are going to have flags all over them," said Peri. "It will be a grand sight to see. We must certainly go."

"We certainly must," said Patter. "We will each take her a red rose from our garden. Red roses mean 'I love you', and

that will show her that there are three people in this village who are fond of her."

So, when the morning came, the three pixies each picked a red rose from their garden. They put a leaf behind each rose. Then they set off to the station. But on the way there Patter and Pipkin found that they had forgotten to put clean hankies into their pockets.

"Bother! We can't go out without clean hankies," said Patter. "We'll go back and get them. You go on, Peri."

So Peri went on by himself. He heard the band playing loudly as he got near the station.

Lady Isabel Dumps arrived just as Peri did. Peri rushed up to her, holding out the red rose.

"I'm sorry you are going, Lady Isabel!" he said.

She took the rose and smelt it.

"Oh, thank you," she said. "How lovely!"

Then she suddenly began to feel about in her pocket and in her bag. "Dear me! Dear me, I've left my nice white gloves on the table. Oh, pixie, do you think you'd

go back and get them for me, please?"

"Certainly, Lady Isabel, certainly!" said Peri, and he rushed off, delighted to do something for the kind old lady.

Now, Patter and Pipkin had found their clean hankies, but Pipkin had remembered that he hadn't given the cats their milk. So Patter had left him pouring out the milk, and he had rushed off to the station, red rose in hand.

He saw Lady Isabel there and went up to her. He gave her the red rose, "I'm sorry you are going, Lady Isabel," he said.

She took the rose and looked rather astonished. "Did you get my gloves?" she asked, in a whisper.

"Gloves?" said Patter, puzzled. "What gloves?"

"Oh, didn't you understand me when I said I had left my white gloves on the table?" said the old lady. "Please go and get them, pixie."

"Of course, certainly, at once!" said Patter politely, and he rushed off to get the gloves. The old lady pinned the second rose beside the first, on the front of her dress.

Now, Pipkin had finished giving the cats their milk and he came rushing to the station, carefully carrying his red rose. He ran up to Lady Isabel Dumps, holding out the rose and panting for breath.

"I'm sorry you are going, Lady Isabel," he said. She stared at him in the greatest surprise. She thought he was the same pixie back again, of course.

"Where are my gloves?" she asked him.

"I beg your pardon?" said Pipkin politely.

"I said, 'Where are my gloves?'" said the old lady, getting impatient. "I want my white gloves that I left on the table. I don't want any more red roses. You keep on giving me them. I want my white gloves."

"Lady Isabel, I will get them for you," said Pipkin, and he rushed off at once. He met Peri coming back. Peri had got the gloves, and he waved them at Pipkin.

Pipkin was astonished to see him. He was even more astonished to meet

189

Patter, who, not being able to find white gloves, had found a pair of red ones.

"Funny," said Pipkin. "Very funny. The old lady must be very fond of gloves."

He rushed to the house where she had been staying but, of course, there were no white gloves on the table. But there was a pair of green ones on the sideboard.

Pipkin snatched them up and raced back to the station.

Peri had given the white gloves to the old lady and she was pleased. Then up rushed Patter and gave her the red ones – and then came Pipkin with the green ones.

All the gloves and the pixies made the Lady Isabel feel rather queer. She looked round the station hurriedly. "Are there – are there any more pixies?" she asked, in a very faint voice.

"We'll fetch some more, madam," said the station-master, thinking she must be fond of them. But the old lady gave a squeal, jumped into her carriage, banged the door, and lay back in her

seat, fanning herself. She didn't want
any more red roses, gloves or pixies!

"Goodbye!" shouted everyone.

"Goodbye!" shouted Peri, Patter
and Pipkin.

The engine whistled. The train
drew out.

"Funny old lady!" said Peri.

"She seemed very fond of gloves,"
said Patter.

"She might have said goodbye to us," said Pipkin.

Well – we'll say goodbye to them instead, shall we? Goodbye, Peri, Patter and Pipkin! See you again another day!